the
bargain

christine s. feldman
author of *coming home*

CRIMSON
ROMANCE
F+W Media, Inc.

This edition published by
Crimson Romance
an imprint of F+W Media, Inc.
10151 Carver Road, Suite 200
Blue Ash, Ohio 45242
www.crimsonromance.com

ISBN 10: 1-4405-6905-3
ISBN 13: 978-1-4405-6905-0
eISBN 10: 1-4405-6906-1
eISBN 13: 978-1-4405-6906-7

*To my wonderful, one-of-a-kind husband; my family; and my friends:
Thanks for your support!
And Mom, Melanie, and Jill…thanks for being my beta readers!*

Chapter One

It was like living in the story of Beauty and the Beast, Shannon decided, something many women probably would think had great potential for romance and happy-ever-after love. Too bad she was cast in the role of the beast.

Sitting cross-legged on the faded floral quilt her grandmother made many years ago, Shannon turned another well-worn page in her high school yearbook and took a cautious sip of her morning coffee, wincing at the heat of it and then blowing on the rest in an effort to spare her mouth from third-degree burns. Somewhere downstairs in her living room was an invitation for her ten-year high school reunion that had recently come in the mail. Its arrival brought a lot of memories to mind, most of which she would rather forget, but there were a few highlights that had driven her to dig out her old yearbooks. The one on her lap was from her senior year.

There weren't very many pictures of her in this particular book beyond the requisite senior picture, which was probably not such a bad thing. She frowned down at the image taken nearly ten years ago. The smile was tight-lipped, hiding the braces from the unforgiving camera.

Ah, well. At least in black and white it wasn't so obvious that her hair looked like an exploding fireball of color. She wasn't interested in her own picture anyway.

Turning the page quickly, she found the face she wanted.

Andrew Kingston.

She traced her fingers over his features. He went by Drew now. Either way suited him, but he thought Drew made him more approachable to his constituents somehow, more boy-next-door. Maybe he was right. What did she really know about politics anyway?

Drew had been class president. Politics was in his blood, and he was good at it, too. The kind of politician who would get things done and keep his promises. She brought the cup to her mouth for another sip of coffee as she contemplated his classically handsome features. And who knew, maybe one day—"Ow!"

Coffee was still too hot. Shannon fanned her open mouth and said a bad word.

Her shaggy mongrel, Bo, cocked an ear at her and gave her a disapproving look.

"Well, it's hot!"

He gave her another look as if to say *duh* before yawning hugely and rolling over on the bed to allow her better access to his belly.

"Subtle," Shannon said, but she obliged him and scratched his stomach with one hand while turning her attention back to Drew's picture. She didn't know why she tortured herself like this. He barely noticed her then, and he barely noticed her now. About the only thing that had changed was now her teeth were straighter, thanks to the hateful braces.

She flipped a few pages back to a place she had turned to so many times before that the pages naturally fell open to it now. A candid picture, students lolling around a grassy knoll of picnic tables at lunchtime, arms around each other's shoulders in a pose for the camera. And right in the center? Drew, of course. Close-cropped hair, broad shoulders, and an even broader grin. A couple of girls on either side smiled adoringly at him instead of at the camera.

There were lots of pictures with Drew in them. And in every picture, he was surrounded by friends—and usually girls. There were plenty of girls carrying a torch for him in high school, and Shannon had been one of them.

"Still am," she murmured ruefully, closing the yearbook. It would have been so much easier to get over him and move on if he were a jerk, but unfortunately he was not. He was kind, intelligent, and as handsome as ever. And so she was basically screwed, because in ten years, give or take, he had never seen her as anything more than "good old Shannon," and it was doubtful he ever would. She could probably show up to work naked, and he would still hand her papers to file without so much as batting an eye. For a moment Shannon let herself indulge in a fantasy in which she showed up to Drew's office wearing something red, revealing, and *highly* inappropriate for work. A smile played on her lips.

Then she glanced at the clock on her nightstand and scrambled off the bed to pull a pair of sensible slacks out from her closet.

Minutes later, she sprinted down the stairs with coffee cup in hand, neatly sidestepping an assortment of tools she neglected to put away last night before dragging her tired body to bed. No matter. She'd need them again tonight to finish the tiling in the kitchen, so really she was just saving herself time this way.

Shannon finished the coffee, fed Bo, and pulled her hair back into its usual braid without needing to look in the mirror to check her handiwork. Grabbing a stack of folders and a breakfast bar, she swung her purse over her shoulder and hurried out the front door.

It was coming along despite what the naysayers told her in the beginning, she thought with some satisfaction as she paused by the side of her truck long enough to give the old house a quick appraisal. Most of the work she had done on the place so far was on the inside to make it more habitable, but the porch was no longer falling apart and the crumbling front steps were no longer a safety hazard. She was better with tools than she was with plants, but maybe she would venture to add a couple baskets of flowers for some color.

It was nothing fancy, but it was hers.

And it was secluded, she thought, starting up the engine and pulling out of the long, graveled driveway. Peaceful. Granted, the extra minutes it took to drive back inside the city limits were a pain—especially when she was on the verge of running late like today—but she loved the quiet solitude that surrounded her place.

Her place. She still had trouble believing it sometimes. Shannon Mahoney, homeowner. Sure, Drew Kingston was still virtually oblivious to her as a woman, but she had come a long way since high school. Now if only she could get him to see it.

Spring weather was turning nicely into summer, and the drive into the city was pleasant. Or it would have been if she took the time to notice it. Her speedometer edged past the posted speed limit when she glanced at her watch, and she forced herself to slow down. Better late than ticketed for speeding, she reminded herself through gritted teeth. With the money she poured into the house lately, she could barely afford gas let alone a ticket. Still, it was with great relief that she turned into the parking lot and saw Drew's sedan was not yet in its spot. Right, she told herself with an inward eye roll, because men are so turned on by punctuality. Oh, well.

She had not, however, beaten Clarissa into work. The woman was twice Shannon's age and still perky enough for both of them. "Morning, Shan!" she said with a cheery wave as she glanced up from her desk in the main office.

"Morning."

The older blonde gave Shannon a once-over and clucked disapprovingly. "Beige, beige, and more beige. Don't you own anything else, honey?"

"Sure. Tan."

"Not funny. There's a nice figure lurking somewhere under those boring old clothes of yours. You only get to be young once, Shannon. You ought to be making the most of it."

"I'm doing just fine."

Clarissa raised one eyebrow. "Are you sure?"

She thought her cheeks might be turning pink, not a good color combination with her hair. "You know what? I think I hear Drew's phone ringing."

"Liar."

Shrugging unapologetically, Shannon beat a hasty retreat and unlocked the door that led to her desk and to Drew's office. It was only a temporary reprieve, she knew. Clarissa's youngest child had gone off to college last fall, and apparently she thought Shannon was as good a means as any to combat empty nest syndrome. It did no good to remind her that Shannon already had parents, thank you very much. They were off enjoying what they liked to call early retirement in Florida—it sounded better than "sitting around unemployed"—and Clarissa clearly felt that such long-distance parenting didn't count. She might be right.

Shannon flipped the lights on and dropped her armload of files on her desk, careful not to let any of their papers spill out. There was a week's worth of work invested in the top one alone, and time was too scarce around here to risk having to redo any of it unnecessarily. Not that she minded the work. She began humming under her breath as she opened the door to Drew's small office and positioned the window blinds to let in the morning sun the way she knew he liked it. She was good at organizing things and being efficient, and she appreciated the steady paycheck. Winding up as assistant to councilman Drew Kingston had been an unexpected bonus.

Bonus? Delight would be a better word.

Drew had not actually been the one to hire her; that honor went to his predecessor. The day newly elected Drew Kingston walked through the door in his perfect suit and matching tie, Shannon decided maybe, just maybe, miracles did occasionally happen to ordinary folks like her.

Sunlight splayed through the blinds and landed on a thin sheaf of official papers on Drew's desktop. She glanced at them in passing. The youth center. Shannon knew those papers backward and forward by now. Drew probably did, too. Was he having second thoughts? She pictured him sitting alone in his office the night before, reviewing everything and wondering if he was really ready to do this. It was his brainchild, but maybe the cost was too personal not to reconsider it at least a little bit. He might be her dream man, but he was still only human, after all.

Returning to her own desk, Shannon tore open the wrapper of her breakfast bar as she glanced at the clock. Budget meeting at ten o'clock, she thought as she took a bite and then opened up the calendar on her computer. The upcoming charity auction... Then there was that zoning issue for him to look at before next Thursday. Anticipating his request, she had already begun to delve into that for him.

The phone rang, interrupting her train of thought. She choked down the bite of dried fruit and granola mixture, trying not to make a face. She really ought to start eating a real breakfast. "Drew Kingston's office," she said with a voice raspy from granola that hadn't quite made it down her throat yet. "How may I help—"

"I want to talk to Drew. Now."

Great, she thought sourly. One of those. Nothing like beginning the day with a surly citizen. "Mr. Kingston is not available at the moment. I could take a message, if you like."

There was a humorless laugh on the other end. "Right. What is that, code for 'he's screening calls'?"

"It means he's not available." Her tone was cool. Even a city councilman got his share of angry callers, and Shannon had no qualms about keeping them at bay.

"Bull. He's hiding in his office, isn't he?"

Her voice got even cooler. "Mr. Kingston *doesn't* hide."

"No? Because it seems like he went out of his way to keep a low profile on this one, sweetheart."

What was this loon talking about?

Forget it. She heard the front door open then and Clarissa greet Drew. He didn't need to start his day out on a sour note like this. "I'm sorry, sir. Mr. Kingston naturally wants to listen to the concerns of constituents, and he values their feedback, but he's very busy at this time. Why don't you call back later and schedule an appointment? Have a very nice day."

"Don't you dare hang—"

She let the phone fall back on the receiver, feeling just a little bit wicked and not the least bit sorry.

"Good morning, Shannon."

As it always did when she saw Drew, her heart tightened a little inside her chest. "Good morning."

Trim and polished, he was what every politician wished they looked like. The suit was expensive but worth every penny since it fit him so well. His shoulders were just as broad as they had been in high school and his body just as lean. Nowadays he had an air of maturity about him that he hadn't quite earned back then, but his smile was still boyish in its charm. "Everything all set for the budget meeting?"

She nodded and held out a file for him.

"Wonderful," he said, looking through it. "Eleven o'clock?"

"Ten."

"Oh, that's right. Thanks. What would I do without you?" Drew smiled again, but it was with less energy than usual.

For the first time, Shannon noticed dark circles under his eyes. "You look tired. Can I get you anything? Some coffee?"

"No, thanks. I've had four cups already. Any more caffeine and I'll be too jittery to hold my pen steady."

She hesitated, wanting to ask if everything was all right but not sure if her asking would make him think she was being too presumptuous somehow. Then he disappeared into his office and closed the door behind him, and the moment was gone.

Coward, she thought to herself.

A short while later she knocked cautiously on his door to deliver a piece of mail to him.

"Come in."

She opened the door to see him seated behind his desk and staring out the window. "Sorry," she said. "This was just messengered over, though, so…"

He nodded toward his desk, and she let the letter fall onto it. Then he went back to staring out the window.

Just say it, she told herself. *Ask* him already. "Is everything all right?" she blurted out finally.

There. She had said it, and miracle of miracles, he didn't look shocked or offended. Was basic conversation this hard for everyone, she wondered, or just for her?

"Oh, sure," he said with a slight sigh and a shrug of his shoulders. "It's just…Do you have any family, Shannon?"

"Me?" she asked, surprised. "I…well, parents. A couple of cousins maybe that I haven't seen in years."

"Parents still living?"

She knew his were not. "Yes."

"That's nice," he said faintly. "No brothers or sisters, though."

"No."

"Mmm," was all he said, and he went back to staring out the window.

Now what? she wondered. Ask him again? Turn around and leave? She froze like a wild animal caught in the headlights of an oncoming car. How could any woman be this inept around a man?

Drew saved her by speaking again. "This youth center…"

"Yes?" she said hopefully.

He turned to look at her and frowned. "Do you think…" He trailed off, his fingers rifling idly through the papers she had spotted earlier on his desk.

"Yes?" she repeated.

But he seemed to think better of whatever he was going to say. "Never mind. I shouldn't be keeping you from your work like this. Don't mind me."

Feeling a little disappointed, Shannon turned to go.

"Oh, Shannon?"

She turned back, hope sparking anew. Would he confide in her after all? Thank her for her concern? Be touched that she cared enough to ask after him?

"Could you do me a favor?"

"Of course. What is it?" *Comfort you? Hold your hand? Have your baby, maybe?*

Drew looked a little sheepish. "I have a dinner date tonight, but I forgot to make reservations. Could you call Le Joli and ask for a table for two? Seven o'clock. Something with a view, preferably."

A pang shot through her, but Shannon kept her expression carefully neutral. "Sure. Anything else?"

"No, that's it, thanks. Good old Shannon. You're a lifesaver." And he treated her to one more charming smile as she closed the door behind her on her way out.

Good old Shannon.

Pulling up the restaurant's number on her computer as she sat down, Shannon wrote herself a note to call them when they opened for lunch. There was nothing surprising about Drew's request. She had done the same thing for him many times before. It just hurt a little more each time she did it.

Good old Shannon wouldn't fit in at a fine French restaurant, she thought with a glance down at her clothes and a slight hitch in her throat. She cleared it quickly. Good old Shannon was not the type of girl a man thought of when he thought of a romantic dinner for two. Good old Shannon wasn't really the type of girl a man thought about at all.

Maybe with the right clothes, a little makeup ...

Her mother's voice popped into her head, her words an echo from some childhood memory. *You can put a pig in satin and pearls, baby, but it won't change the fact that a pig is still a pig.*

Now where had that come from? she wondered, frowning as she struggled to remember. Her mother had never been insensitive enough to actually imply Shannon bore any kind of resemblance to a pig. Her memory cleared. No, it was back in high school when Shannon had started talking about maybe going to college after all. Her bewildered parents hadn't seen much point to it. They certainly hadn't understood why she bothered to put herself through night school. Come to think of it, there were a lot of things they didn't understand.

Which could be one reason why she didn't call Florida very often.

But for just a moment, sitting there, aching over Drew's obliviousness to her, Shannon found herself wishing her mother were a little closer than Florida. Well, she would wish that if her mother were a little more like June Cleaver and a little less like Peg Bundy—or at least a little more like Clarissa.

"Clarissa?" she called out through her open door.

"Yes?" the other woman's voice floated back to her.

"Want to adopt me?"

"Sure thing, honey."

Shannon smiled faintly and forced her attention away from Drew and onto her work. This was hardly a productive line of thinking. Time to get back to zoning issues.

She made very little headway amid phone calls and emails that kept interrupting her, but she did her best to shut out both the distraction in her heart and the chatter between Clarissa and the occasional visitor. Her eyes were glued to her computer screen, so she couldn't help but let out a startled gasp when a pair of large masculine hands came down on her desktop, one on either side of her computer.

She looked up to see just who had invaded her personal space so abruptly.

"Hello," said a dark-haired, dark-eyed personification of sin. "Remember me? I believe you hung up on me earlier."

Chapter Two

The first thought that went through Shannon's head was, dear Lord, I hope he doesn't have a gun.

The next was to wonder how anyone could possibly look that good outside of the pages of a magazine.

And the third one was to wonder why he looked vaguely familiar to her. With features Michelangelo might have chiseled and a mouth to die for, he could have easily been a movie star or a model. Maybe she really had seen him in a magazine somewhere. The only trace of a flaw in his face would be the dark shadows beneath his eyes, lending him a vaguely troubled look that worked quite well for him.

Those eyes darkened further. "Interesting choice in phone etiquette for a secretary—"

"Personal assistant," Shannon corrected him coolly, struggling both to regain her composure and to place just where exactly she had seen this man before.

He leaned closer to get eye to eye with her, a move she was sure was calculated. "Sweetheart, you can slap whatever label on it you like. I really don't care. What I do care about is getting in to see your boss, right now."

Magnificent or not, he did not get to come in here and try to bully his way past her. "And as I explained to you on the phone earlier," Shannon said, slowly and purposefully standing up so that he couldn't tower quite so much over her, "Mr. Kingston is a very busy man with a very busy schedule. You can't just walk in without an appointment."

"Hard to make an appointment when you're left talking to a dial tone, isn't it?"

Her face grew a little warmer, and she knew her cheeks were turning unbecomingly pink again. Wonderful. "If you're going to behave like a childish brat," she said primly, "don't be surprised if people treat you like one."

"Oh, you are a charmer, aren't you?"

She ignored that. "I'm sorry, but I believe you've wasted your time *and* mine in coming down here. Mr. Kingston has a meeting starting shortly and can't take the time to see anyone else just now."

The man straightened. "He can make time for his brother."

"His brother?" The fog surrounding her memory finally cleared as things clicked into place. Yes, she vaguely remembered Drew having a brother in school. Marcus? Micah? No, wait... "You're... Michael."

Michael. A few years older than Drew—and therefore Shannon. He was a senior when they were freshmen, and he only existed on the peripheral of Shannon's life since Drew was the center of her universe then, and he and his brother ran in very different circles.

"Heard of me, have you? I'm surprised Drew would think me worth mentioning." There was a slight edge to his voice. She couldn't tell if it was bitterness or sarcasm.

Drew *hadn't* mentioned his brother to Shannon, not even once. But she felt reluctant to explain how she knew of him, almost as if by doing so it would relegate her back to the same wallflower status that belonged to her in high school. Because while she might vaguely remember him, he clearly had no idea who she was.

Michael Kingston. Even if you never spoke to him in school, you knew who he was. To say he had a reputation would be putting it mildly. No respect for authority, unruly and unpredictable. She thought he might have even been kicked out of school at some point. But he was wildly popular. Every girl wanted him, and many got to have him—for a little while. A player was what

Shannon would have called him. Sex-on-a-stick was what many others said instead. And giggled.

In fact, the odds were very good that Shannon was the only girl at McKinley High who hadn't carried some kind of torch for him. If rumors could be believed, that might have included one or two of the teachers, too. But her awareness of him hadn't extended much farther than his relationship to Drew.

"What?" he asked her irritably all of a sudden, and Shannon realized she had been staring blankly at him. Or maybe through him.

She hesitated uncertainly. "I don't think Drew—er, Mr. Kingston is expecting you. He would have said something."

"No, I'm sure this will be the surprise of the decade. But never mind that. Let's get this family reunion started." Michael stepped around Shannon's desk and would have no doubt reached for the doorknob to Drew's office, but Shannon scrambled up and intercepted him. He did a double take, clearly startled to find her between him and the door.

"I don't care if you're his long-lost fairy godmother. You can't just barge in because you feel like it." Pompous jerk, she added mentally.

She had a feeling he was thinking a few unflattering things about her as well. His eyes narrowed. "Move."

"No."

He frowned at her, his frustration showing on his face. "Don't think I won't pick you up and move you myself."

"Don't think I won't kick you where it will really hurt."

Her words made him blink. "You little—"

Before he could finish whatever he was about to say, the door to Drew's office opened and the younger of the two brothers stepped out. "That's enough, Michael."

Shannon's heart did a flip-flop inside her chest as Drew put his hand on her arm to gently move her aside, and she had a feeling she was blushing again. If she was, Drew didn't seem to notice. Story of her life.

"If you've got something to say, you can say it to me, not to Shannon," Drew told his brother tersely.

"I've been trying to," Michael returned, the edge back in his voice as he spared a brief and aggravated glance toward Shannon. She frowned back. "Easier said than done."

"What do you want, Michael?"

"What do I want? I want you to quit screening your damn calls, for starters, and pick up the phone when I call you. I want you to remember that our parents had two sons, not just one." He pulled a crumpled newspaper clipping from his pocket and held it up in front of Drew's face. "And I want to know where you get off pulling a stunt like this!"

Unable to help herself, Shannon strained to see the headline. She couldn't make it out, but she did recognize the building in the black-and-white photograph that accompanied it. Kingston Manor, the old family home and the future housing of the Kingston Youth Center.

"Kept it out of the bigger newspapers so far, haven't you? I'll bet you didn't think I would find out," Michael continued, his anger growing. "At least not until it was too late to do anything about it. Am I right?"

For the first time, Drew looked a little uncomfortable, maybe even slightly embarrassed. "This doesn't concern you, Michael."

"The hell it doesn't! It was my home once, too."

"That was a *long* time ago." Drew's voice grew cooler.

A shadow crossed Michael's face. "Oh, I get it. I walked out, so—"

"*Ran* out is more like it."

In the midst of the heated exchange, Shannon glanced toward the outer hall to see Clarissa watching, her mouth open in surprise.

The blonde mouthed the words *what's going on?* Shannon gave her head one furtive and bewildered shake.

"So, what…I'm not a Kingston anymore? And here I thought family was supposed to be everything to you. Or maybe that's only when you're campaigning."

"Don't pretend to care about family now. It's too little too late." Michael thrust the article at him. "Drew, this is a mistake—"

Drew snatched the article from his brother's hand and crumpled it up. "That's not your call to make."

A new voice interrupted them. "Excuse me—"

Everyone turned to see a beefy man in a security guard uniform standing in the hallway.

He cleared his throat pointedly and adjusted the belt from which hung a substantial-looking nightstick. "Is there a problem here, Mr. Kingston?"

"Not anymore, Lucas. This gentleman was just leaving. Maybe you could help him find his way out of the building, though?"

"Drew, we have to talk about this!" There was something else besides anger beneath Michael's words, something so faint that Shannon wondered if she might have imagined it. Desperation, maybe? She didn't think Drew noticed it.

"We're done talking," Drew returned coldly. "We were done a long time ago. Now, please, Lucas?"

The security guard nodded. "Absolutely, sir. Right this way, please." He reached for Michael's arm.

Michael shook him off. "*Don't* put your hands on me."

Lucas curled one hand around the handle of his nightstick.

For a moment Shannon thought Michael was going to hit either Drew or Lucas, but a tiny gasp from Clarissa seemed to remind him where he was and just who was around him. The fist he was starting to form slowly relaxed.

"I'll find my own way out." With a final glance at his brother, Michael turned and stormed out of the room. Lucas followed him out.

Drew turned to Shannon and shook his head with a rueful sigh. "I'm sorry, Shannon. You shouldn't have had to deal with any of that. Are you all right?"

She nodded, self-conscious again as he focused his attention on her.

"It's not that Michael's dangerous or anything, not really. He's just impulsive. Says what he wants, does what he wants, without giving much thought to the consequences. You know what I mean?"

Another nod. Could she not think of two words to say to him?

"Again, I'm sorry." He turned as if to go back into his office.

Shannon finally found her voice. "Are *you* okay?"

He paused and then ran a hand through his hair, leaving it slightly mussed but still boyishly charming. "Oh, sure. Just caught me off guard, that's all. He's been trying to call me at home recently, but I never dreamed he'd actually come back to town. Seeing him out of the blue like that..."

"How long has it been?"

"Years. Not since our parents' funeral. We didn't exactly get along then, either."

"Sorry," she offered awkwardly but sincerely.

He waved it off. "It is what it is. Michael's always been one for trouble, and I suspect he always will be."

"Do you think he'll come back here?"

Drew frowned, but not at Shannon. "Not here, he won't. I'll speak to the security staff about him. Hopefully he'll get the hint and leave town quickly." He gave a humorless chuckle. "It's what he's best at." Then he glanced at the clock on the wall. "I'd better get to that meeting. Let's just try and forget this morning's unpleasantness, shall we?" Retrieving a handful of papers from his desk, he smiled at Shannon a little too brightly and disappeared down the hall.

As soon as he was gone, Clarissa hurried over to Shannon. "What on earth was that all about?"

"Something about the youth center, apparently." Shannon sat down behind her computer again determined to follow Drew's advice and forget about Michael Kingston's visit. Easier said than done. Her pulse was going faster than it usually did.

"I didn't even know Drew *had* a brother."

"He says they're not close." She thought back to high school. "I'm not sure they ever have been."

The older woman raised her eyebrows. "Wait a minute. Did you used to know him or something?"

"Who, Michael?" Shannon shrugged, disinterested. She brought up a new file on her computer, only half-involved in the conversation. "I knew *of* him, that's all. Back in school."

Clarissa sat on the edge of the desk. "Spill it! I love a little gossip. What was he like?"

Shannon hesitated. They were treading on dangerous ground here. Talk about Michael could very easily lead to talk about Drew. If she wasn't careful, she might let something slip about her feelings for him. "I don't know. Probably not so different from the way he is now. Tall, dark, and entitled."

"Oooo, but he is easy on the eyes, isn't he?"

"Clarissa!"

"What? I'm married, not dead. And I'd have to be dead not to notice a man like that." She fanned herself with her hand. "My goodness! And a bad boy to boot. Every woman's kryptonite."

Not every woman's, Shannon thought. Some preferred nice, polite politician types.

"I'll bet girls chased after him like kids after an ice cream truck." She lowered her voice slyly. "So did he let them catch him?"

"I wouldn't really know."

"Oh, come on," Clarissa pleaded hopefully. "Are you sure you don't know any juicy stories?"

"Sorry."

The blonde sighed with disappointment before returning to her desk.

It was funny, Shannon thought as she started typing. You would think two men who were brothers would have a little more in common, but these two hardly even looked alike. There were some similarities, she supposed. The noses, the chins…But Drew's hair was straight where Michael's was curly. Drew's eyes were a warm shade of blue while Michael's were—She struggled to remember. Brown, maybe. Almost black. Definitely dark.

The note she had written to remind herself to make dinner reservations for Drew and a date caught her attention, and she decided the smart thing to do was to stop thinking about Drew's eyes.

• • •

Michael peeled off his much-scuffed leather jacket and tossed it onto the ground beneath a large oak tree using more force than was necessary. Taking a seat on the shady grass beneath its overhanging branches, he turned stony eyes to the door of the building in which his brother worked.

That could have gone better. Well, it was hardly the first time he managed to screw things up, and it was a safe bet that it wouldn't be the last time, either. He ought to know better than to let his emotions plot the course instead of his head, but knowing and doing were two very different things, weren't they?

The security guard was ever so helpful in making sure he did indeed find the exit all right and even took the time to explain in no uncertain terms that Michael would not be seeing the inside of Drew's building again anytime soon. So now not only could he not get Drew to take his calls at home—and the doorman at his brother's high-rise apartment complex was about as helpful as that carrot-topped battle axe in the office—but now his work was closed off to him, too. Wonderful. He was fast running out of options through which to reach Drew and fix this mess that the younger Kingston was in the process of creating.

Michael sank back against the trunk of the tree and rubbed eyes that were weary from too many hours on the road and not enough caffeine. He had lost his temper in there, a stupid thing to do. It was hardly the best way to get Drew to see his point of view. Granted, the exchange with the secretary hadn't exactly helped his frame of mind, but that was only a small part of it. His head hadn't been right ever since he stumbled onto that article about the family home and the highly touted youth center Drew planned to make out of it. Drew must have been astonished that Michael had seen it. He would probably be even more shocked if he knew that his older black sheep of a brother actually checked up on his former hometown every once in a great while. It wouldn't occur to him that Michael would care. But there were a lot of things that Drew didn't know about him anymore and probably wouldn't believe. Like the regrets.

If he could just get Drew to listen to him with an open mind for two minutes ...

Not likely. Michael chuckled bitterly under his breath, startling a matronly passerby. He flashed her a quick smile of apology, and she blushed before smiling back and ducking her head to continue past him.

Now *she* would have let him in to his brother's office, no doubt about it. Too bad she hadn't been the one to intercept him in there.

But what was done was done. If he couldn't get his brother to listen to him, maybe he could get through to someone else to make them reconsider things. Now if there happened to be a female on the committee involved in this project, he might stand a chance. Desperate times, and all that. A man used whatever weapons he had in his arsenal.

He remained in the shade of the tree for quite awhile as he mused over possible strategies, maybe even hoping to catch his brother coming outside, when the doors to the building opened and a familiar figure emerged. His jaw tightened.

The battle axe.

She looked deceptively mild at the moment, from her plain, thick braid to the tips of her sensible shoes. Even the purse slung over her arm looked mild, a simple and unembellished brown thing. Just went to show you, Michael thought, appearances really can be deceiving. He couldn't remember the last time a woman spoke to him the way she did. Maybe not since grade school. Give her a ruler, and she would probably rap his knuckles.

He wondered if she really would have kicked him.

If he'd kept his head instead of arguing with her, laid on a little charm, things would have gone very differently, he was sure. She might have swung the office door open wide instead of growling at him like a mama bear protecting her cub. This was obviously not a woman who cared to hear anything negative about the perfect Drew Kingston.

He remembered then the blush that came to her cheeks when his brother appeared. The way she clammed up, suddenly shy. One side of Michael's mouth curved up in a smile of dawning comprehension. Ah, that explained quite a bit. The battle axe had a thing for his brother. Michael might not be the classically educated university man that Drew was, but women were his favorite subject, after all, and he knew them very well. This woman clearly had a crush on Drew. He knew his brother well, too, and it was equally obvious to him that Drew had no clue about her feelings for him.

An idea began to take shape in his mind, and Michael leaned forward to watch the secretary—no, she preferred to be called assistant, didn't she?—walk down the sidewalk. Sure, it would take some sweet-talking at first after what happened this morning, but he was good at that. He had never met a woman yet who wasn't at least partially susceptible to his charms, especially when he turned them on full force. They had gotten him out of more than one bind in the past. An apology for this morning, some mild flirtation, and once she warmed to him, he would make a proposition he doubted she would refuse.

Hope flickered to life. Getting to his feet, Michael slung his jacket over one shoulder and followed her.

• • •

Eleven o'clock was a little early to be taking her lunch break, but Shannon's stomach had been growling since about five minutes after finishing that sad, little breakfast bar. There were a number of cozy coffee shops and undiscovered little eatery gems within easy walking distance of the office, and today she headed for one of her favorites, a charming little Italian place whose warm and rustic colors had done much to inspire her kitchen remodel. Brown-bagging it would have been more practical and definitely cheaper, but since she planned to finish the tiling tonight, it seemed fitting to celebrate by eating at the same place where it all began, inspiration-wise at least.

Her favorite table was available, a secluded corner spot beneath a lovely fresco. She let her purse fall gently onto the table and then sat down. "Iced tea and minestrone, please," she called out as a familiar waitress waved in greeting.

"Make that two," said a voice that made her stiffen, and she looked up to see Michael Kingston sliding into the chair across from her. "Hi."

She stared at him with wide eyes, bewildered first and then annoyed. "What are *you* doing here?"

"Eating lunch. And trying to apologize." He smiled at her, a slow, boyish smile that invited her to join in his good humor. She chose not to but only stared at him in cool silence. "Look," he continued when it became clear she was not going to thaw out that quickly, "clearly we got off on the wrong foot back there, and I know that was largely my fault." He paused and looked at her as if waiting for her to reassure him that was not the case.

Then he would be waiting a very long time, she thought, still staring at him with undisguised hostility.

Apparently he realized that because he finally shrugged and went on. "I was upset with my brother, and I took it out on you. But family can make everyone a little crazy sometimes, right? That's just the nature of—"

"What do you want?" she asked bluntly.

He raised his eyebrows. "Direct, aren't you?"

The waitress appeared with their soup and iced tea, and she bestowed a particularly sunny smile on Michael. He favored her with one in return before giving his attention back to Shannon. Probably can't even help himself, she thought, unimpressed.

"I want your help," he said finally.

"*My* help?" Was he kidding?

"You're Drew's sec—personal assistant," he corrected himself before she could. He paused to taste his soup and possibly consider his next words. "And I'm sure you have his ear, at least to some degree. You're like the gatekeeper between him and everyone on the outside. I need your help in getting through to him."

"Is this a joke?"

"No joke. Drew's about to make a big mistake, and I want you to help me stop him—Hey, this is really good soup. Aren't you going to try yours?"

Shannon left her food untouched, incredulous. "What makes you think I would stab Drew in the back like that? Particularly for you?"

For a moment he looked annoyed. "It's not stabbing him in the back. All I want you to do is talk to him. You'd be saving him from himself, actually."

"And I'm supposed to believe that because you say so?"

"I'm his brother. I wouldn't do something that might hurt him."

"Right. Because you two are so close."

"We're family. Blood means something."

Blood meant something to sharks, too, she thought. "Forget it. Get lost and let me eat my lunch, please."

"You can at least think about it. You help me, and I'll help you."

Now she was really confused. Where was he going with this? "Help me? What are you talking about?"

"I saw the way you looked at my brother."

Shannon blinked, and then her face grew hot. "What?"

"Look—it's Shannon, right? There's no reason why we can't both get what we want here." Michael leaned back and flashed her another very attractive smile. Across the room, their waitress sighed audibly. "So can we talk?"

Shannon slowly pushed her chair back from the table and stood up.

"At least think about it?" Michael urged her.

"Oh, believe me, I will think about this." Picking up her bowl of minestrone, Shannon dumped it in his lap before slinging her purse over her shoulder and storming toward the door. "Lunch is on him today," she called to the open-mouthed waitress over her shoulder as she left.

• • •

On the plus side, the soup was not as hot as it could have been, Michael thought as he tried to wipe off the worst of it with his napkin. "Towel, please?" he asked the shocked waitress politely through gritted teeth, and she hastened to get him one.

That could have gone better, too.

Chapter Three

If she thought he would give up that easily, she was in for a surprise. Thanks to the soup, Michael had sacrificed a favorite pair of jeans and a little of his dignity, but that was hardly enough to scare him off. Humble him, maybe, but not scare him. Cockiness would not impress this woman. Neither would charm. Maybe honesty would. If that didn't work, perhaps he would give groveling a try.

It wasn't hard to find out her last name. He might not be allowed inside the building, but that didn't stop him from striking up a conversation outside with a giggly young thing who worked there and who loved to chat. After that it was a simple matter of looking one Shannon Mahoney up in the phone book.

He decided two things before he went to pay her a visit. First, it would be best to wait a couple of days until the weekend so she would have time to cool off. Second, it would be wiser not to call ahead, given their history on the phone together. A peace offering of some sort might not be a bad idea, either, but he had a feeling she wouldn't be impressed by the typical bouquet of flowers. Besides, some flowers had thorns, and he didn't want to give her anything she might be able to use as a weapon against him.

This time he didn't bother trying to rehearse strategy or practice speeches in advance. He had a feeling doing so would only cause more harm than good. Shannon Mahoney didn't seem to fit the mold of other women he had known in his life, so everything he thought he knew about the opposite sex was out the window in her case. Which meant he was essentially going in blind, but few options were open to him at this point. He would have to gamble on earning her goodwill.

He tried not to let that thought discourage him.

Her address lay well outside of the city limits, and the area here was unfamiliar to him. As a teenager, he preferred to see what trouble could be found in town. And then the moment he turned eighteen, he had walked out the door and left it all behind him. Or at least he thought he had.

He missed the turnoff for her road at first and had to double back to find it. She must really like the country, he decided. The only signs of civilization he saw on this particular road were the telephone poles and wires that bordered it. Somehow it didn't come as a shock to him that she might possibly be a bit of a hermit who preferred to stay as far away from other people as possible. He was a little surprised not to see No Trespassing signs up when he turned his truck onto her winding gravel driveway.

The house was a very old one, but it was obvious someone had been restoring it. The white paint on the exterior looked new, as did the railings on the front porch. A couple of ceramic flowerpots sat on either end of the top step, new additions by the looks of them. The bright crimson petunia plants in them looked too small to have been in the pots for very long. Somehow the cheerful color they lent to the porch came as a surprise to him. There was something so…he struggled to think of the right word. Hopeful, he thought finally. There was something happy and hopeful about them that he had not expected from Miss Mahoney.

There was another truck parked there already, so he assumed she was home. Excellent. He pulled up next to it and got out, one hand around the Styrofoam container that held his peace offering. He had taken only three steps when a large shaggy dog of mixed heritage came trotting around from the back of the house. Michael froze. Of course she would have a dog, and it was probably trained to take a bite out of strangers who were foolish enough to stop by without calling first. He glanced back at his truck, trying to decide if his best option was to dive for the truck bed or simply stand still and hope for the best.

But the dog only wagged his tail and tried to sniff at the Styrofoam container in Michael's hand.

Michael let out the breath he was holding and sheepishly rubbed the dog behind the ears with his free hand. Some shining example of masculinity he was, nearly treed by Snoopy. "Sorry, this isn't for you, pal. Where's the lady of the house?"

The words were barely out of his mouth when the serene silence of the morning air was broken by what sounded like the buzz of a power saw. It seemed to come from behind the house. The dog trotted in the direction of the noise, and Michael followed.

He rounded the back of the old house and saw a pile of lumber, a half-finished deck, and Shannon with a pair of safety goggles on and a hefty circular saw in one hand. Her fiery hair was pulled back in a ponytail to keep it out of her face, but it was so thick and full that she kept having to flip the ends of it back over her shoulder. The plain but functional office work clothes from before had been replaced by plain but functional denim overalls and an oversized T-shirt.

Unaware of his presence, she finished trimming off the end of a piece of wood that was suspended on two sawhorses, then held up the saw as she let the power cut out. The spinning blade glinted in the sunlight as it slowly lost speed. He stared at it uneasily.

This might have been a very bad idea.

• • •

It was too early in the morning for her to feel this hot already. Chalk it up to a little manual labor, she supposed. Shannon pulled off her safety goggles and raised her arm to wipe the sweat from her forehead.

Bo barked at her.

"What is it this time, Bo? Squirrel or rabbit?" Then she glanced up and saw that it was neither. Her mouth fell open at the sight of Michael Kingston standing in her backyard with some sort of package in one hand and the other resting on her "loyal" companion's furry head. His observation about the way she looked at Drew immediately popped back into her head, and she felt a fresh burst of humiliation wash over her. She decided anger was preferable to humiliation and let it help her find her voice. "You've got to be kidding me. What are *you* doing here?"

Michael took off his sunglasses and tucked them over the collar of his plain black T-shirt, his expression serious. "I'm sorry about the other day, but I need to talk to you. Please."

"No. Go away."

"I will if you just promise to hear me out first."

"You're lousy at taking a hint, you know that? Am I being too subtle? Because I could take it up a notch."

He remained where he was, despite eyeing her power tools with noticeable unease. "Five minutes is all I'm asking. Look, I know I acted like a jerk when we first met, and I am sorry. I was frustrated and having a bad day—bad week, really. Are you going to tell me that's never happened to you?"

Sure, it had. She'd had plenty of bad days, including the day he showed up. "Okay, fine. If I forgive you, will you leave?"

The corner of his mouth twitched as if he was trying not to smile. "I have to say, I've never met a woman as eager to get rid of me as you are."

No doubt. He made a very pretty picture in the sunlight, and his T-shirt did a nice job of showing off the fine physique he had beneath it. Even the trace of stubble on his face couldn't have been more perfect. He probably couldn't look ugly if he tried. "I can believe that," she muttered under her breath, trying to hold on to her anger but finding it harder to do the longer he stood there looking all humble and contrite like that. Probably just an act, she cautioned herself, so don't let your guard down.

He took a cautious step forward, his free hand held up in a gesture of peace. "I'm sorry if I made you uncomfortable before. I didn't mean to embarrass or offend you with what I said about you and Drew, I swear. And your secret's safe with me, if that's the way you want it." He looked rueful. "Come on, he won't talk to me anyway. You've got nothing to worry about."

She knew her cheeks looked like two bright roses again. Raising her chin higher, she did her best to look disdainful. "I never said you were right about any of that, did I?"

The look on his face spoke volumes. *You didn't have to.* But he only shrugged agreeably. "No, of course not. But my offer to help is still on the table if you're interested in making a deal here."

Hopefully he couldn't see how much his words tempted her.

His eyes fixed on the circular saw in her hand. "Hey, could you at least put that saw down? You're making me a little nervous."

That would have been reason enough for her to keep a good hold on it, but it was pretty heavy, and her arm was getting tired. Giving him a look to let him know that his feelings had little bearing on the matter, she nevertheless set the saw down on the ground, unplugging it as a safety precaution.

"Thank you. I appreciate it." With the power tool safely out of play, Michael closed the rest of the distance between them with more confidence. "Here," he said amicably, holding out the package in his hand. "For you. Peace offering."

Now that she could see it better, Shannon realized that it was a Styrofoam container with a lid on it, the kind a person might carry food or drink in. It was certainly too wide to be a coffee cup. She frowned, wary. "What is it?"

"Minestrone. You never got to eat yours the other day."

She stared at him, trying to see if he was joking or actually serious. "You made minestrone?"

"Hell no, I bought it. I can't even make a decent sandwich, let alone anything that needs cooking. I'd appreciate it if you wouldn't make me wear it this time."

This time she was sure there was a hint of humor in his eyes. She had to admit it wasn't unattractive. "No promises."

Michael set it on the finished part of the deck, pushing it out of her immediate reach with a sidelong look and a raised eyebrow.

She felt a little flicker in her stomach that she squelched immediately. Oh, he was a cute one, all right. It was lucky for her that she was immune to him. "Whatever it is you think you want from me, don't count on getting it. I told you before I wouldn't betray Drew's trust, and I meant it."

"Good. I'm glad he has someone like you in his corner. Despite the fact that he and I can't seem to be in the same room together without wanting to knock each other's teeth out, he is my kid brother. What I want from you is something that's in his best interest anyway. So, will you hear me out?"

He sounded earnest enough, and her anger had cooled to a minor sort of bristling. "You have five minutes, starting now," Shannon said, deciding it would be best to avoid looking at him directly, kind of like protecting her eyes by not staring into the sun. She began cleaning up the various bits of lumber she had trimmed off this morning, turning her back to him.

"Okay. I need you to help me stop Drew from making a big mistake."

"Yeah, you mentioned that last time. You know, your brother has a pretty good head on his shoulders. Just what mistake is it that you think he's making?"

"The youth center. I'm sure it sounds good in theory, but I don't think he's thought it all the way through. Hey, is this thing okay to sit on?"

Shannon glanced around and saw him testing the strength of her half-finished deck with one hand. "Of course it is," she answered shortly, feeling a defensiveness born of too many run-ins with good old boys who assumed a woman couldn't possibly tackle home improvement projects by herself. "I know what I'm doing."

He looked up at her, surprised. "I wasn't implying that you don't. I just thought it would be good manners to get your permission first. See? I'm being a good boy today."

"Oh," she said, nonplussed. "Then, yes, you can sit there."

He settled onto it and ran his hand along the smooth wood of her workmanship. "Nice," he commented. "I'm very impressed. I have trouble even putting a picture frame up on a wall."

"Trying to kiss up?"

He grinned slowly. "Well, now, if kissing will help…"

She reminded herself quickly that she disliked him, even as his words made her pulse speed up unexpectedly. Well, like Clarissa said, a woman would have to be dead not to notice a man like Michael Kingston. Perfection had to be acknowledged, whatever form it took. "You're down to four minutes now," she said stiffly.

"Fine. Drew wants to create a place for underprivileged kids to get help with their homework, play sports, and all kinds of other good things. That's a great idea. If he wants to do that, I'm all for it. Just not at Kingston Manor."

Shannon started to open her mouth to protest.

He held up his hand quickly. "Before you call me a snob or tell me to get lost again, let me explain. I'm the last person that place would mean anything to, and that probably makes me sound like a huge hypocrite when I say this now, but that place is full of my family's heritage—Drew's heritage. It was built from the ground up by a Kingston, and it's been in the family for generations. It should stay that way."

She was instantly suspicious. An estate like that was worth an awful lot of money, after all. "Why? If you're hoping to find any legal loopholes, you're in for a big disappointment. Drew's had lawyers prepare everything very carefully, and your parents left Kingston Manor to your brother free and clear. If you're planning on swooping in and getting your own hands on the place—"

"I don't give a damn about any of that!" he said with a vehemence that surprised her into silence. "And I don't want the place for me. I don't belong there, and I never did. I want it for *him*."

"You want it for him," she repeated doubtfully, not sure what he meant.

"Yes. One day my brother will have a family of his own. He was born to be a family man, and I have zero doubt he'll be a model dad. Little League, PTA—he'll do it all. He'll have kids to carry on the family name, the family traditions. He should hang on to the place for their sakes, if nothing else."

"You really expect me to buy that? That this is all because you want to be uncle of the year to some kids that haven't even been born yet, and you're all about family now? Forget it. Your reputation precedes you."

Her words seemed to hit him much harder than she expected, and she almost felt a little guilty at the stricken look on his face. Almost. After a moment, he nodded tersely. "Yeah, I've screwed up a lot with my family. I can't change the past, though, can I? That's why the future matters so much."

"And the money that house represents means nothing to you."

"I don't need the money. I have my own place, my own business. I didn't take money from them then, and I don't want any of it now."

It was plausible, she supposed, studying him. Then again, it could be the biggest load of bull someone had ever tried to sell her. If it weren't for the look she had just seen cross his face, she would have written him off entirely. At the end of the day, though, she didn't care to be a pawn in any game he might be playing. "Maybe you're telling the truth, and maybe you're not. Either way, I really don't think it's something I want to get mixed up in." She bent down to plug the saw back in.

"Not even for Drew's sake?"

She froze at first and then straightened, avoiding his eyes. They saw her feelings for his brother too clearly for her liking and recognized her Achilles' heel. "I think Drew will be just fine."

"Why gamble on that, though? Where's the harm in just talking to him? I'm just asking you to make the same points with him that I made with you. You could end up saving him from a lifetime of regret. But if he thinks the whole thing through and he's one hundred percent sure the youth center is still what he wants to do, then…" He trailed off, and his face betrayed signs of an inward struggle she didn't understand.

"Then what?" she persisted, wondering what was really going on inside his head.

He didn't answer her immediately, and when he finally did, his answer did nothing to reveal what he was thinking. "Then I guess I'll have to live with that."

That wasn't enough to satisfy her. "Why?" she asked, making eye contact with him again and staring at him hard this time as if by doing so she would be able to read his mind. "Why is this so important to you? What do you get out of it?"

"It's not about me, it's about Drew."

Right. His body practically radiated tension. "Oh, I think it's a little about you, too."

He shrugged, tight-lipped, and she knew she wouldn't get anything more from him, at least not today. It was tempting to tell him to get lost then, but if she did that, who knew what other avenue he might take with the youth center? If she agreed to do what he asked, she would at least be in the loop if some sort of ulterior motives showed up later.

Where's the harm in just talking to him?

His words echoed in her head. The request seemed harmless enough on the surface. It might even be helpful to Drew, as Michael suggested. And maybe Michael really could help her get Drew to notice her —

No, no. She wouldn't let that be a factor in her decision, she decided firmly, trying to ignore the way her heart seemed to beat a little faster at the thought. At least not consciously, she wouldn't. Drew deserved better than that. *She* was better than that. "Okay," she said finally, slowly getting the words out and half-wishing she could take them back. "Maybe—*maybe* I believe you're on the level with all of this."

Michael's head shot up, and the hopeful look on his face actually made her determination to dislike him waver slightly. "So does that mean—"

"I don't know what it means yet," she said irritably, appalled at the fleeting softness she felt toward him. She was definitely off her game here. "I guess it means I'll think about it."

Suddenly he was right in front of her, making her draw in a sharp breath of surprise. He put his hands on her shoulders, and she wondered with fleeting panic—or was it possibly anticipation?— if he was going to hug her. This was, after all, Michael Kingston, the lady-killer of McKinley High. Many women would happily commit felonies just to have him put his hands on them, even in such an innocent way as this. "I can't ask for more than that. Thank you."

She took a step back from him before she could start blushing or, worse, stammering. "Yeah, sure. Fine."

"Call me when you've thought it over. Got a pen? I'll give you my cell phone number." He spotted a ballpoint pen she'd been using to mark measurements on the lumber and picked it up. "Here, give me your hand."

Hesitantly, Shannon held out one hand and tried not to jump when he took hold of it to write his number down on her palm.

She really was inept around men, apparently even the ones she didn't like all that much.

"I'm staying at a motel in the city. The Piedmont Place—kind of a dive, but cheap. You could leave me a message there, too, if you can't get through to my cell."

She only half heard him, distracted by the feel of her hand in his very warm one. Her fingers must seem awfully stiff to him, but despite her best efforts, she could not will them to relax. Did he notice?

If he did, he was careful to avoid showing it. Probably wouldn't want to risk blowing the tentative agreement they had reached. He handed her pen back to her. "I think my five minutes were up a while ago. Thanks for letting me say my piece."

She shrugged, feeling awkward as usual. "I'm not making any promises."

"I understand." Michael gave Bo one last scratch behind the ears. "You really should try the soup. It's good stuff."

"I know. It's even better when you eat it."

He blinked and then started to smile. "Well, well. She jokes. The world is full of possibilities today." Then he put his sunglasses back on and started walking back the way he had come.

Shannon caught herself staring at the way his jeans fit him so well and forced herself to look away. She glanced at the phone number on her hand and then met Bo's eyes. "What?" she demanded defensively. "I'm a big girl, and I know what I'm doing."

She hoped.

• • •

Michael emerged from behind the house without the company of a canine escort this time, and as he walked back to his truck his step was lighter than it had been before.

Finally. Finally there was a reason to hope he might be able to fix things. Well, he thought with a pang, as much they could be fixed. Some things couldn't be undone no matter what he did now. But for the first time in recent weeks, Michael felt as if a weight might be lifting from his shoulders. It had been there for a long time, way before he ever saw the article about Drew's plans for the family home. Certainly since his parents' funeral. Granted, Shannon hadn't agreed to do more than just think about helping him yet, but they at least seemed to be on better terms now.

Their truce was a fragile one, though. He didn't dare push his luck and hound her any further, which meant he was essentially stuck waiting by the phone and praying that Somebody up there took pity on him. He had never been good at waiting, and now when there was so much riding on one woman's decision, it was likely to be sheer torture. Distraction was the logical course of action, but a man could only play so many games of pool before getting a little restless. *Right*, Michael thought with a self-deprecating laugh. Restless. He'd passed restless years ago and was well on his way to someplace darker than that.

He chose to change his train of thought.

Stopping by the driver's side of his truck, he glanced back the way he had come.

Shannon Mahoney. She was an interesting creature, and one that was hard for him to figure out. Sharp-tongued and handy with power tools one moment, but then blushing and awkward the next. It made for an unusual combination, one that he'd never seen in a woman before. There was something almost, well... *likeable* about it. And she was loyal, too. That much was clear. She could be good for his brother, if unconventional. He could honor their deal and help her win Drew over with a clear conscience, if she chose to enter into it.

He grinned, remembering the look she gave him when he asked her to put down the power saw. Then again, she might be too much for Drew to handle.

...

The deck remained unfinished by the end of the day, but it wouldn't be too long before she had it done if she kept plugging away at it. Then she could sit outside on quiet weekend mornings and absorb the sounds of nature while sipping from a hot cup of coffee. Well, at least when Bo wasn't chasing nature away.

She would have gotten more of the deck done today, but her mind was preoccupied after Michael's visit. In fact, she ruined a couple of perfectly good pieces of lumber simply by not paying attention to what she was doing and then cutting them the wrong lengths.

Showered now and lounging comfortably on her bed with her legs criss-crossed yoga-style, she leafed through her collection of high school yearbooks, starting with the one from her freshman year—and Michael's senior year. There weren't many pictures of him in it, almost as if he purposely avoided the camera. Even in his senior picture, he looked as if he'd rather be anywhere but there, which resulted in a brooding sort of expression that—naturally— looked good on him.

And now she was contemplating teaming up with the ultimate bad boy of her high school years.

Should she do it? He seemed sincere enough, and he said all he wanted was for her to talk to Drew, to just get him to consider Michael's perspective. It seemed safe enough. She tried to think it over from every possible angle, even a few ridiculous ones that would have made any conspiracy theorist proud, and she still couldn't come up with a solid reason why it would be a bad thing for her to do.

She recalled then the relief on his face when she said she would think about his offer, and she felt an unexpected softness toward him then, mild but there nonetheless. Well, she could feel a little bit of sympathy without really liking him, she supposed.

Leafing through the pages of the yearbook, she found Drew's freshman picture. She couldn't resist smiling at it. Few boys could pull off the age of fourteen with any great degree of suavity, including Drew. He had a gangliness to him then but still wore the same smile that could make her heart go all aflutter now.

Her good humor faded as she remembered his hesitation a few days ago in his office and the question he almost asked her about the youth center. He was conflicted about some aspect of it. Maybe he even shared some of Michael's doubts about the future of the family home.

In that case, Michael could be right. Talking to him about the youth center might be in his best interest after all, before he finalized plans that couldn't be taken back and then wound up with one big pile of regrets.

That realization finally helped her come to a decision.

Reaching for the phone, she punched in the number Michael gave her earlier.

He answered after the first ring. "Hello?"

"It's Shannon."

"So have you decided?" he asked, and she could practically hear him holding his breath as he waited for her answer.

She took a deep breath of her own and plunged ahead. "Are you free for lunch tomorrow? And by the way, you're buying."

Chapter Four

Michael forced himself to stop after his third cup of coffee. Shouldn't she be here already? He checked his watch again. No, she wasn't late yet, and the minute hand hadn't moved any farther than the last time he checked. He needed to relax. Either that or his watch needed a new battery.

He leaned back in his chair and glanced yet again out of the coffee shop window. It felt almost like first-date jitters, which was ridiculous because Michael was not a man who experienced those kinds of jitters. But most men didn't have as much riding on a date as he had riding on this little meeting. He had tried calling Drew at home again this morning and was not surprised when it went straight to the machine. Drew wrote him off a long time ago. If Shannon decided this was a bad idea after all, he might as well roll out the welcome mat for the Kingston Youth Center.

A flash of color caught his eye through the window: that blazing hair of hers. He had the impression that she was always struggling to tame it, and today she had done so by pulling it up into a tight and prim sort of bun. His fingers twitched as if grasping at imaginary hairpins. Shannon Mahoney might benefit from letting her hair down in more ways than one. He tried to imagine her relaxed and laughing but couldn't.

She finished parking her truck and got out, pausing to wait until traffic had cleared enough for her to cross the street. Michael leaned forward and studied her with new interest. Clearly she believed in dressing low key, given the plain sort of clothes he'd seen her in the few times they'd met, but the jeans she wore today hugged her hips much better than anything else he'd seen her in. And the T-shirt was not oversized this time. Well, well. Miss Mahoney had a pretty damn good figure lurking under there. Who knew?

"You know what?" he greeted her as she came through the coffee shop door and spotted him. "You're really not a bad looking woman."

She stared at him, and then her cheeks turned rosy. "Gee, thanks. I'm touched. Is that your idea of 'hello'?"

"It was supposed to be a compliment."

"Needs work."

"Duly noted."

Still looking vaguely put out, Shannon pulled out the chair across from him and sat down. There was a menu on the table, and she chose to look at it instead of at him.

Michael leaned forward, studying her more closely. "I'm serious. You play it down a lot—or maybe you just don't know how to play it up—but the foundation is all there." It was true. Full lips, clear skin—except for a light dusting of freckles that gave her a girlish look—and blue-green eyes that were flashing with irritation at the moment. "With a little effort, you could turn heads. Including Drew's."

She still didn't look pleased with him. The blush was coming back, though. Truth be told, he got a kick out of how easy it was to make her blush.

He tried again to win her over. "This is good news. Smile, would you?"

"I'm not comfortable with this line of conversation," she said stiffly.

"Sweetheart, you'd better get comfortable. Men notice things like a woman's mouth or her body. If you're not comfortable talking about them, how are you ever going to be comfortable *doing* anything with them?"

Oh, yes. She was turning a darker shade of red by the second. No wonder she was awkward around Drew.

He felt a flicker of pity for her. "Fine. We'll table that conversation for another time."

"Oh, goody."

"So you've thought things over...Are you on board?"

She didn't answer right away but looked at him with such intensity that he could swear his body temperature began to rise. "Look me in the eyes and tell me one more time that you're not here to cause problems for Drew or screw him out of his inheritance."

Was that why she wanted to meet face-to-face today? To see if she could spot something about him that would set off warning bells? Well, for once in his life he had right on his side. He put his hands on the tabletop and leaned in closer to show he had nothing to hide. "I swear," he said slowly and deliberately, his eyes never leaving hers, "that I am here to protect my family's interests, that's all. And Drew's all the family I have left now. Satisfied? Or did you bring a Bible for me to swear on?"

"Maybe I should have. I still think there's more to this than you're telling me."

"Will you talk to Drew or not?"

After a long moment, Shannon nodded, but she didn't look all that happy with her decision. "I'll talk to Drew, nothing more. So don't try to slip in any changes to the deal later."

"Understood."

"And if he says no, you'll walk away."

Her words made his gut twist. He tried not to let it show on his face, because she was still watching him closely. "I will."

Some of the tension in her body finally lessened. "Okay, then."

"So we've got a deal?" Michael held out his right hand expectantly.

She eyed it with undisguised reluctance but put her own hand out to shake it.

He closed his fingers around hers and tried not to smile when she tensed up. "Would you relax? You haven't made a deal with the devil, I swear."

"We'll see," she muttered, taking her hand back. She started to push her chair away from the table and stand up.

"Where are you going?"

"We don't need to actually eat lunch together. I just wanted to be sure before I said yes to anything, and I'm as sure as I'm going to be."

"So you're going to make me eat alone? That's just cruel."

Shannon looked a little confused, or maybe wary. "You *want* me to stay? I find that a little hard to believe."

Actually, he found exchanging barbs with her was something he was starting to enjoy. Did that make him a sadist or a masochist? he wondered. "We've still got a few things to talk about."

"Like what?"

"Sit down and find out."

Frowning, she hesitated, but after a moment she sat down again.

A young man with a crew cut and an apron stopped by their table. "Hi!" he greeted them brightly as he pulled a pen out from behind his ear and grabbed an order pad from his pocket. "Have you decided what you want?"

Michael thought he heard Shannon mumble something under her breath that sounded a lot like "I hope so," but he pretended he hadn't. "Burger," he said instead. "Medium rare with the works."

"And for the lady?"

"House salad," Shannon said flatly. "I don't have much of an appetite this morning."

The waiter smiled and left, and Michael ran his hand over his forehead in a gesture of relief.

Shannon frowned. "What?"

"No soup today. The world is a safer place."

Was it his imagination, or did the corners of her mouth twitch slightly as if she was trying not to smile? She might just be warming up to him after all—not much but a little bit, he thought. Maybe it was the challenge she represented, but he realized with some surprise that he wanted Shannon Mahoney to like him. Or at least not to dislike him so much.

Well, he could make the first step by honoring his end of the deal. "Now that we're partners," he said, leaning in again, "we should talk about my end of the bargain. Helping you with Drew."

"I…that's not necessary."

"A deal's a deal. We shook on it and everything. I may be a lot of things, but I'm not someone who goes back on his word."

She shook her head with a wan smile. "Thanks for the offer, but I don't think I'd feel comfortable with it."

"With what?"

"With…manipulating Drew."

"Who's manipulating? I'll just give you a few pointers on what guys like, that's all. Think of me as your own personal advice columnist. Is there something shady about what they do?"

"Well no."

"So?" She hesitated, and he marveled at the ethical dilemma she seemed to be having. Most of the women he'd met in his life had no problems whatsoever with blatant exploitation of whatever advantages presented themselves to them. This particular female defied all his expectations. "You want to get Drew's attention, right?"

Shannon sat frozen like a deer in headlights.

"It's all right to say it."

Finally, she nodded. Once.

He felt that flicker again, like sympathy maybe. Who knew? He was in unfamiliar territory with this woman. "Then today is lesson one in how to win your guy. Forget what they say about the way to a man's heart being through his stomach, okay?"

She rolled her eyes. "Oh, please. I know exactly what you're going to say. Something about the way she fills out her clothes, right? Or maybe about her bedroom skills? This is your profound bit of wisdom for me?"

"No."

"No?"

"Sure, men like a woman with a good body. Don't women like a man with a good body?"

She folded her arms across her chest. "I'm sure you already know the answer to that question."

"Well, thank you, Shannon. I'm flattered you think of me that way."

"No, wait, I didn't mean—"

"But a great body alone will get you nowhere," he continued, unable to keep from grinning at the discomfited look on her face. "Oh, it'll get you some attention, but in order to hold it, you need something else."

The waiter appeared then with their lunches, and Michael sat back so he could slide his burger in front of him. "Enjoy," the young man offered, setting Shannon's salad down before her.

Michael picked up his burger with both hands and took a large bite. He glanced at Shannon while he chewed. She didn't touch her salad but only watched him expectantly. He took another bite and chewed it very deliberately.

"Well?" she asked impatiently.

There was something about her that made him unable to resist teasing her. "What?"

"Unless your super secret tip to lure a guy in has something to do with that burger, you haven't given me much to work with."

"Oh, that. All right, here it is." He set the burger down and leaned closer to her, lowering his voice to a conspiratorial whisper as he did so. He didn't think she realized she leaned in, too. "The secret thing that men find irresistible has nothing to do with looks or clothes or the latest hairstyles. The thing no man can truly resist is confidence."

"Confidence."

He leaned back again and took another bite. "Yes."

"That's it?"

"Hey, don't knock it. A man sees a woman who walks like she knows she's got it all, and he can't resist going after her to find out if it's true. I'm telling you, there is nothing sexier, and I've known quite a few sexy women in my life. Next time you go to some big party or something with lots of people, take a really good look around at the women who are the center of attention. More often than not you'll see they aren't knockouts, at least not in the classical sense. They've got something much, much better."

"Confidence," she repeated again, sounding less than confident as she said it.

"Yes," he agreed. "And I won't lie to you, it's hard to fake if you don't already have it to begin with."

"So, in other words, I'm screwed yet again."

He knew what she was thinking. *Thanks for nothing.* "No," he said, more gently this time as he sensed her rising frustration. "It just means you're going to have to work to bring it out a little more. But, deep down, you've got it. You just need to set it free."

She made a derisive sound beneath her breath and finally began picking at her salad.

Michael was no stranger to flattery, but it rankled him that she seemed to assume that was all his words were. "What? You think I'm just blowing smoke here?"

"Well, what am I supposed to think? You saw me in there the other day. I turned into a bumbling mute the moment Drew appeared, and that was actually one of my better days."

She looked so forlorn sitting across from him. He had an inexplicable urge to make her feel better about herself. "So you're awkward in social situations. We can work on that. But, trust me, Shannon, you've got moxie to spare."

Those blue-green eyes of hers looked up at him in surprise. They were nice eyes when they weren't full of hostility or suspicion. Very nice.

Michael lost his train of thought for a moment and had to force it back on track. Confidence, he reminded himself. That was what they were talking about. "I mean it," he continued finally, feeling awkward and not liking the unfamiliar sensation of it. It made him put a little more bite into his words than he intended. "You just have to learn to channel it into other things besides minestrone and chainsaws."

One side of her mouth curved up slightly, and if she noticed the bite, she didn't seem bothered by it. "Circular saws."

"Yeah, those, too."

Her smile grew, and it even looked as though she was trying not to laugh.

He had succeeded in cheering her up. Funny how that made him feel better about himself, too.

• • •

"So why Drew?"

Shannon finished the last bite of her salad and glanced up. "What do you mean?"

"Of all the men in all the world, why is he the one you want?"

She was beginning to lose her self-consciousness about the matter, around Michael anyway, at least to the point where she no longer felt her face grow warm when he mentioned it. That had to be some progress. "Are you really so surprised? He's got a lot of female admirers." She should know since she was the one making his dinner reservations for him.

Michael had already finished his burger and now sat back in his chair and studied her while he idly picked at the French fries that came on the side. Something flickered briefly in his expression that might have been irritation. "But what is it about him? Looks? Money? Sense of civic duty?"

Apparently she hadn't completely gotten over being self-conscious. Poking at one last little part of a lettuce leaf on her plate, she avoided Michael's eyes. "I don't know. The whole package, I guess. He's just a really great guy."

"Saint Drew. I've heard this story before."

She frowned at him. "I never said he was a saint, but is there something wrong with being a good guy?"

Michael gave a small, rueful chuckle. "No, not a thing." He turned his face to look out the window, his expression distant. "It just sets the bar awfully high for sinners like me."

She wondered if he would explain what he meant by that, but he remained silent. She didn't think he was just trying to be cute. "You almost sound like you're feeling sorry for yourself."

He turned back to her, startled. After a moment a wry smile spread across his face. "Me? Never. Somehow I doubt you would let me get away with that." Clearing his throat, he pushed his plate of French fries toward her. "Here. Have some."

They did look tempting in all their greasy glory. She let him change the subject and reached for one. "Thanks."

"How long have you had a thing for my brother?"

And we're back to that, she thought. She squirmed inwardly. "Does it matter?"

"Maybe, maybe not. Depending upon how long you've known him, you may want to approach things differently." He put a French fry in his mouth.

She mumbled something under her breath.

"I'm sorry, what?"

"I said, about ten years. Give or take." It was a conservative estimate, but he didn't really need to know that, she decided.

Michael nearly choked on his fry. "*Ten years?*"

It was hard not to sound defensive. In fact, she was sure she failed completely. "Something wrong with that?"

"No, but...Damn. Ten years and you've never told him how you feel about him?"

She gave him a dark look and ate another of his French fries.

"I'm sorry, it's just a little hard for me to wrap my head around." He stared at her thoughtfully. "Maybe I underestimated my brother."

"What do you mean?"

"I mean, I don't think *I've* ever inspired feelings with that kind of longevity in a woman."

She frowned, trying to tell if he was making fun of her or not. No, she decided finally. He looked genuinely shocked and possibly a little pensive. She took pity on him. "Oh, you never know."

Michael glanced up at her, looking as surprised as she felt at her words.

Now where had that come from? she wondered, carefully refocusing her attention on the fries. Since when did she care if Michael Kingston felt bad about something? It must be basic human decency, she told herself. Or maybe she was going soft.

In any case, he let it go unaddressed, for which she was grateful. "So, ten years...That would take it all the way back to high school, wouldn't it?"

She nodded, still very deliberately working on getting just the right amount of ketchup on her fry so she wouldn't have to look at him.

"Wait—were you and Drew in the same graduating class?"

"Yeah."

"Then that would mean...so you and I were actually in school together?"

"For a year, yes."

He gave her a very thorough once-over as if trying to place her. "You and I—we never hooked up in high school, did we?"

Shannon's mouth fell open. "No, we certainly did not!"

"So is that why you were really so mad at me the other day?"

"What?" she sputtered hotly. "You are unbelievable!"

"Oh, so we *did* hook up."

"You—"

A slow grin spread across his face, and she realized he was playing with her.

Taking a deep breath, she bit back a name she had been about to call him. "You get a perverse pleasure out of yanking my chain, don't you?"

"Kind of, yes."

"Aren't you afraid I might back out of the deal?"

"No, I think you realize it's in Drew's best interest. Besides," he added with a knowing gleam in his eye, "I think *you* get a perverse pleasure out of putting me back in my place, so we're developing a great little symbiotic relationship here. Don't you agree?"

"What? Oh, I'm sorry. I'm still recovering from the shock of hearing such big words come out of your mouth."

Michael started to laugh, and Shannon felt a kind of rush go through her. He might be right when he said she enjoyed taking him down a peg. There was something exhilarating about feeling so free to speak her mind to somebody the way she did with him.

"I definitely would have remembered you if we ever did cross paths in school," Michael said finally.

"Drew doesn't," she admitted ruefully.

"Drew doesn't know you went to McKinley High?"

"Doesn't seem to, no."

He frowned, looking confused. "I thought you said—"

"I knew who *he* was, but we didn't exactly run in the same circles. I think he spoke to me a sum total of three times during our four years there. And then after that I didn't see him again until he became a city councilman."

"So you've been carrying a torch for him based on a few sentences in high school? Don't you think you may have built your feelings for him up a little too much?"

"No! And quit making me sound like a stalker. I didn't follow him around or anything. He was class president, for Pete's sake. Quarterback on the football team. Prom King. He was out front and center for everyone to see along with the type of person he was. Drew never picked on any of the other kids, never cheated on a test—"

"Sure, that you *know* of."

She ignored him. "A lot of girls liked him. Then when he became a councilman and my boss, I just…well, I just realized that old feelings die hard, okay?"

"Okay, but why haven't you ever mentioned to him that you went to school together? Seems like it would be a natural opener."

"I wasn't exactly the most popular person in high school, all right? In fact, it was kind of a nightmare for me, and one I'd just as soon not relive. If he doesn't remember the geek I used to be, why remind him?"

"That bad?"

"Girls can be catty. Let's just leave it at that."

He looked like he wanted to ask her something more, but he let it drop. "High school is hell for everybody," he said instead.

Shannon raised her eyebrows. "Yeah, right. Not for you."

Michael looked out the window again. "You'd be surprised."

• • •

Lunch was over. There were no more French fries to eat, and no reason to linger any longer. Still, Michael wasn't in as big a hurry to leave as he thought he would be. "So you'll talk to Drew this week?" he asked as Shannon started to get up from the table to leave.

"I'll try."

"He doesn't have a ton of time left to reconsider things." Even he could hear the undercurrent of tension he had tried to keep out of his voice. He made an effort to keep his expression neutral. Easier said than done, judging by the slight softening he saw in Shannon's face as she looked at him.

"I understand." She hesitated and then added, "I mean it. Okay?"

He believed her. "Sorry. Just anxious, I guess."

She nodded, not with a lot of warmth maybe but without any perceivable traces of antagonism either.

"Call me after?" he asked as she headed for the door. If he weren't careful, he was going to make a real pest of himself. He bit his tongue to keep from blurting anything else out.

"I will." She let the door swing shut behind her.

Michael watched her walk a short way down the street before crossing it. All in all, he thought things had gone well. She was going to help him, and he realized he actually wanted to help her. Startling though it may be, Shannon Mahoney was growing on him. He might even go so far as to say he was starting to like her. The mouth on her …

He tried hard to picture her in high school but couldn't. It was highly unlikely they had ever crossed paths at McKinley, but he wondered what would have happened if they had. He almost wished they did.

He saw her start to pull open the door of her truck and then pause. Something had caught her attention, but he couldn't tell what. Curious, he leaned closer to the coffee shop window to see better.

She was looking at a window display in a women's clothing store. There was a dress of some kind. It might have been green, but the sun's glare off the glass made it difficult to see much. It was definitely short, though.

A smile made his lips curve. "Do it," he urged beneath his breath. "Take a walk on the wild side, Shannon."

Almost as if she could hear him, she shook her head and pulled the truck door open all the way.

"Do it," he whispered.

She paused again, and then Michael's grin got wider as she slammed the door shut and walked toward the store.

"That's my girl."

• • •

This was a mistake, Shannon thought, standing in the middle of the boutique surrounded by rack after rack of clothes she would never have the nerve to wear in public and almost certainly couldn't afford. What had possessed her to come in here?

She turned around to leave but stopped with her hand on the door.

Confidence. A woman of confidence would not let tiny things like shopping or dressing room lighting intimidate her. A woman of confidence would take a chance on something new, especially when the old had not been working out so well for her. And she most certainly wouldn't have a panic attack at the thought of showing off a little skin. Would she?

Then clearly she was not a woman of confidence yet. Baby steps, she told herself and peeled her fingers off the door handle.

Forcing herself to take slow, deep breaths, Shannon put one foot in front of the other until she was standing before a saleswoman who was putting together a trendy ensemble for a mannequin.

The woman, chic from the cutting edge style of her bobbed hairdo to the tips of her stiletto heels, looked up with a practiced smile pasted to her face. "Hello. Welcome to Martinique's."

"Help me," Shannon said.

The saleswoman's eyes widened as she took in Shannon's jeans and T-shirt, but then she laid a well-manicured and comforting hand on Shannon's shoulder. "Girlfriend, you've come to the right place." She smiled, a gleam of anticipation in her eyes. This is going to be fun."

Chapter Five

"Why would any woman want to torture herself like this?"

Oh, sure, the spiky heels looked cute and sexy when she wasn't actually trying to walk in them. Any sophistication they lent her was ruined the moment Shannon tried to take a step.

She stumbled around her bedroom, practicing, hoping she would get the hang of them before she left for work in five minutes. At this point, she was not very optimistic about reaching that goal.

Bo whined anxiously and watched her progress, or lack of it.

"Don't worry, Mommy's fine," Shannon assured him, and then nearly proved herself a liar by pitching forward and catching herself at the last minute on the bedpost.

At least at work she would be sitting most of the time. That is, if this skinny little pencil skirt would allow it. Choosing to take the stairs in her stocking feet to be on the safe side, she carried the new shoes in one hand.

Twenty minutes later, walking up the steps at the entrance to her workplace went a little more smoothly than her attempts at home. As long as she held on to the railing and took small steps, she moved with halfway decent grace. Small steps to the door, small steps over the threshold —

A woman's shriek startled her into nearly losing her balance again. Shannon quickly clutched at the doorframe for support as she started to wobble. "What the—"

Clarissa came running to greet her, her hands on her cheeks and her mouth hanging open. "Oh my stars! Who are you, and what have you done with Shannon Mahoney?" She put her hands on Shannon's shoulders and looked her over from head to toe, eyes shining with undisguised delight. "Eeek! I love it!"

"Clarissa, you nearly gave me a heart attack."

"Me? What about you? I don't think I've ever seen you in a skirt before. You've got legs! It's like invasion of the body snatchers or something."

"Yeah, well, I'd better not drop anything today, because in these heels and this skirt—" She tried unsuccessfully to inhale deeply and failed as the waistband refused to let her. "I don't think I could bend over and make it back up again."

"Maybe not, but you'd look great trying. Oh, Shannon, what came over you?"

She knew she radiated anything but confidence. "Temporary insanity?"

"Then you should go crazy more often. And, honey, that shade of blue looks beautiful on you."

Glancing down a little shyly, Shannon smoothed out nonexistent wrinkles in the silky top. "I don't know. It's a little too…something."

"Non-beige? That's its nicest feature, dear. Trust me, you look wonderful." Clarissa took a step back to review her one more time, then frowned at Shannon's hair. "But, honey, why don't you let your hair out of that braid for once? As long as you're trying a new look and all."

"No, I think it's better the way it is. Really." She had briefly considered cutting it or getting someone to change the color for her, but then lost her nerve. She had tried that once before, years ago, and wound up slinking out of the salon with green hair. It was not an experience she was in a hurry to repeat.

Apparently Clarissa was satisfied with her answer, because she didn't press the matter. Instead, she gave Shannon a quick hug. "Well, you look lovely, my dear."

"Thank you."

"I mean it. Oh, look! Doesn't Shannon look wonderful today?" she said to someone behind Shannon.

Self-conscious, Shannon turned around to see Drew walking through the open doorway, briefcase in one hand and cup of coffee in the other. Confidence, she reminded herself and forced her shoulders back. "Good morning."

The double take Drew did was probably the loveliest thing she had ever seen in her life. "Good morning. You do look...wow. Special occasion today?"

"I...I'm, uh—" Her mind drew a blank, and she blurted out the first thing that popped into her head. "Well, I'm meeting someone after work." Great. Were confident women liars, too? "I mean, I might be. You know, later." Oh, just stop talking, she thought harshly at herself.

"You have a date?" Clarissa squealed happily. "Who's the guy?"

See, this was why it was a bad idea to lie, Shannon thought with growing tension. Besides the guilt it induced, it tended to snowball. "Um, well, I don't..."

Clarissa looked suddenly wary. "It's a blind date, isn't it? Be careful there, honey. In this day and age you never know who might wind up sitting across the table from you."

"I'll keep that in mind," Shannon agreed, and she hurried away from the blonde and her questions as fast as her new shoes would allow her. "Excuse me."

"I expect to hear all the juicy details tomorrow," Clarissa called after her.

Well, she would just have to worry about that tomorrow, she thought as she opened the door to her desk and Drew's office.

"You're not going to call in sick tomorrow just to avoid her, are you?"

Drew's voice right behind her made her jump slightly. "What? Oh." She smiled nervously. "Don't tempt me."

He grinned back. "Because I have a feeling she would only track you down."

"You could be right."

He continued past her to his office door. "Well, whoever the guy is, he's going to be very impressed when he sees you walk in tonight."

"Thank you." She sat down at her desk as he disappeared into his office, and then she let out the breath she hadn't realized she was holding. Worth every penny, she decided, fingering her new clothes as she turned on her computer.

She was not quite so enthusiastic about them a couple of hours later when she grew tired of breathing shallowly to accommodate the skirt. Her balance in heels was improving a little, but her poor pinched toes protested every time she got up to move around. Whenever possible, she slipped the shoes off her feet and let them recuperate in hiding underneath her desk. It was just the first day of wearing them, she reminded herself. Surely it would get easier.

In any case, it was probably time to start tackling her end of the bargain with Michael. She waited hopefully for the perfect opportunity to present itself to broach the subject of the youth center with Drew, but nothing seemed quite right. She was honest enough to admit to herself it was probably because her nervousness made her reluctant to recognize such an opportunity.

All right, fine. She was chicken. Maybe pretending she wasn't was the best substitution she could conjure up right now. Michael seemed to think she had moxie. Maybe she really did, buried inside herself somewhere. So what would a gutsy woman do in this situation?

She would *make* an opportunity instead of waiting around for one, Shannon thought.

So without allowing herself time to potentially back out, she got up from her desk and knocked on Drew's door.

"Come in," he called out.

"Hi," she said as she opened the door, trying very hard to make her voice sound breezy and casual. Her mind latched onto the first thing that popped into it. "Just wanted to remind you about that benefit tomorrow night. See if you're all set, or if you have any questions about your part in it. You know, schedule-wise or anything."

"No, no," he answered, glancing up from some paperwork on his desk and looking a little surprised. "I'm ready to go. Thank you."

"Okay, just checking." She stood in the open doorway, wrestling with opening lines.

"Was there something else?"

"I was…I was just wondering about something."

"Yes?"

"It's about the youth center. Last week, you seemed…well, I thought maybe you seemed a little concerned about it."

"Ah. That." He dropped the paper he was holding onto the desk and leaned back in his chair. "It was on my mind, yes."

"Are you having second thoughts?"

He frowned. "What do you mean?"

"Well, it has been in your family for a long time, hasn't it? Anyone could understand why it might be hard to give it up."

For a moment, he didn't answer her, and she wondered if she had inadvertently offended him somehow. But then he shook his head and smiled a half-hearted smile. "The past is in the past. I prefer to focus on the future."

"Sure, but—" Shannon took two steps forward into the room and caught the toe of her shoe on a snag in the rug. She gasped and fell forward, catching herself on the edge of Drew's desk just as he started to rise to help her. "Sorry," she mumbled, wishing the floor would open up beneath her and swallow her whole. "New shoes."

"Of course," he said politely, offering her a hand as she pulled herself upright.

So much for cool and confident. The phone on her desk rang, and she was grateful for the chance to escape. "I'd better, you know…" She gestured toward the ringing phone.

"Absolutely. Just—take it slowly." He flashed her a quick smile and bent over his papers again.

Shannon stepped carefully out of the room, covering her face with one hand as soon as the door was shut. Smooth as silk, Shannon, she thought sarcastically. Kicking the offending shoes off and under her desk, she answered the phone.

There was no more talk about the youth center that day. Drew had a late lunch with business colleagues, the phone kept ringing, and Shannon found making eye contact with Drew difficult anyway after the fall in his office. At least she could honestly say to Michael that she had introduced the topic.

"Have fun on your date tonight," Clarissa told her with a friendly wave as Shannon left at the end of the day.

And speaking of honesty …

Technically, she had said only that she was meeting someone, right? So as long as she actually met with somebody, it wasn't a total lie. And since she promised Michael she would keep him informed, dropping by his motel long enough to let him know the ball was rolling—albeit slowly—would fit the bill just fine. She searched her memory and came up with the name of his motel. The Piedmont Place. She would swing by on her way home.

•••

A knock on his door startled Michael out of his thoughts, which was just as well. They weren't very happy thoughts. He put the picture of his parents he had been looking at in the drawer of the nightstand and went to answer the knock.

"Shannon," he greeted her with surprise, and he let his gaze travel up the full length of her. A tight skirt and body-skimming shirt confirmed what he had suspected the other day: Nice legs, nice hips—nice everything, really. His eyes finally met hers. "What are you doing here?"

"Hi," she said, sounding somewhat wilted. "I should have called first. Sorry."

"No, it's not a problem. I'm just surprised." He opened the door wider and stepped back to let her enter. "Come on in."

"Boy, you weren't kidding about this place being a dive, were you?" she commented as she stepped inside the room with a wary look around. Faded wallpaper was beginning to peel in places, and there was precious little furniture in the room. What little there was didn't match.

"Yeah, it's old. But it's clean, if you're wondering about whether or not to sit down." He waved an inviting hand at the lone chair in the room, a vinyl-covered lump with stuffing poking free in places, and she sat down in it. "Been shopping, have you?"

She slipped off her shoes, wincing as she did so. "A little, yes."

"Looks good on you."

"Too bad it doesn't feel better. I'll take jeans over this kind of stuff any day, and my feet are killing me."

Michael sat down on the edge of the bed nearest to her. "Rough day at the office, dear?"

She rubbed one stocking-clad foot with the other. "You could say that."

He caught himself staring at her legs and quickly looked back up again before she could notice. "I could rub your feet for you."

Most women he offered foot rubs to seemed pleased. Shannon only looked alarmed, and maybe a little suspicious. "No, thank you. You don't have to brownnose, you know. I've already agreed to help you."

"I like to hedge my bets, but suit yourself. I'd offer you a stiff drink, but everything around here comes out of a vending machine." He started to rise from the bed. "But if you want a soda—"

"No, that's okay. I didn't drop by for a drink. I'm basically here so you can make an honest woman out of me."

"Are you proposing? I think you're supposed to be on one knee."

"Ha, ha. I panicked at work and blurted out something about meeting someone after hours. Now that I'm here, it's not technically a lie, see?"

"I feel so used."

"But I also came by to tell you I did bring up the youth center with Drew. It's not much yet, but it's a start."

She had his full attention. "And?"

"And...that's pretty much it. He doesn't seem completely thrilled with giving up the family home, but he insists he's fine with it."

"You're not giving up already, are you?" Michael asked quickly. "I mean—"

"No, no," she assured him. "I just didn't get to talk to him much today." Her cheeks blossomed faintly.

Shannon Mahoney would make a lousy poker player, he thought to himself at the telltale color in her face. "Uh, oh. Something happened, didn't it?"

Sighing, she played with the hem of her skirt and shrugged.

"What? He didn't like your shiny new clothes? Come on, tell me."

"I tripped and fell on his desk," she admitted finally.

He tried not to smile, but it was a struggle. She looked so glum right now, he didn't think she'd appreciate being told that there was something kind of appealing about her awkwardness. "I'm sure it wasn't as bad as you think."

"I *fell* on his *desk*."

"Could have been worse. You could have tripped and fallen in his lap." He pursed his lips thoughtfully. "Actually, that might have been better."

She gave him a dark look. "This isn't funny."

He put on his most somber and sympathetic expression. "Sorry."

"Liar." Shannon slumped further back into the sorry excuse for a chair. "I just get so nervous around him that I have trouble stringing more than three words together, and I do stupid things."

"You don't seem to have that trouble with me," Michael pointed out.

"That's because I don't like you," she replied absently.

"Gee, thanks."

She looked startled. "No—I mean I'm not trying to impress you. Oh, you know what I mean."

"So does that kind of thing happen a lot with you?"

"What kind of thing?"

"Getting nervous around men."

"Oh. Maybe." She averted her eyes, appearing suddenly interested in the view outside his window. Since that view consisted primarily of a row of trashcans and graffiti, he wasn't fooled.

He eyed her speculatively. "Look, if I say something, do you promise not to hurt me?"

Her eyes narrowed suspiciously as she turned back to him. "No."

"Then I'll have to chance it. You strike me as a woman who hasn't had a whole lot of experience with men. Am I right?"

Her mouth dropped open. "I beg your pardon?"

"I don't mean it as any kind of insult. You're a good-looking woman, and you could certainly have an active dating life if you wanted, but I'm guessing your nerves have gotten in the way of that. If I'm wrong, say so."

The fact that she didn't correct him, combined with the fact she didn't try to throw anything at him made him think he had hit it on the nose. But she did look a little embarrassed, and possibly even hurt, and he immediately felt like the world's biggest jerk.

He hastened to fix things. "Hey, I'm serious. There's nothing wrong with you at all except for maybe a little social anxiety. Hell, I've been checking out your legs ever since you got here, and I would be happy to ogle you further if that's what it takes to convince you."

"That's so thoughtful of you." But a flicker of dry humor had replaced the mortified look in her eyes.

"The point I was trying to make was that if you had a little more experience with men, you probably wouldn't be so nervous around them. Take me, for example. I've had plenty of experience with women by now, and I don't even remember the last time I was nervous around one."

"Is this supposed to help me somehow, or did you just want to take a minute to boast about what a stud you are?"

"Some other day maybe. I really don't think we'd have the time it would take right now." He grinned as she rolled her eyes. Yes, she was feeling better. "Listen, I have an idea."

"Why am I suddenly nervous?"

"Hey, nobody said learning how to interact with the opposite sex would be easy. So you don't have much experience with men. You need to start racking some up now, the sooner the better."

Her eyes widened. "What exactly are you suggesting?"

"I'm not suggesting you start bed-hopping, so you can relax your grip on that chair before you snap its arms off. Just go up and talk to some guy on the street. Strike up a conversation at the bus stop. Don't shrink away next time a man stands close to you or brushes your hand accidentally in the elevator."

"I don't shrink!"

"Really?" He held his hand out. "Here. Give me your foot."

She drew back. "What? Why?"

"See? Shrinking."

"I wasn't—" Shannon paused. "Okay, so maybe I was. Why do you want my foot?"

"We're going to do a little social experiment."

"With my foot?" she asked, incredulous.

"I'm renewing my offer of a free foot massage. Nothing better than free."

The blush was back. "I don't think so."

Michael raised his eyebrows. "Because it involves physical contact? It's just a foot massage. Your feet, my hands. That's all."

Despite his assurances, she looked doubtful. Either she was even more inexperienced with men than he originally imagined, or else she was picking up on some kind of big bad wolf vibe he didn't realize he'd been sending out. He softened his voice just in case it was the latter.

"Sweetheart, if you get nervous with me, a man—and I quote— you don't even like, how do you expect to get near a man you *do* like without turning into a quivering mass of jelly? I'm trying to help you here. Just consider this practice."

After a long hesitation, Shannon finally, daintily, edged one foot toward him.

He waited patiently for her to place her foot in his hand instead of taking it himself, suspecting it might only make her more skittish. It was a bit like coaxing a wild animal to come to him, and any sudden movements could scare her away. When she tentatively gave her foot to him, he began to knead its arch very lightly with his fingers.

Her entire leg was rigid with tension.

"Relax. I promise I won't bite," he assured her. "Unless, of course, you're into that sort of thing."

She threw him a look.

He gave her a slow spreading smile, and he thought just maybe she almost let herself return it. "Scout's honor, I will be a perfect gentleman. I'm just trying to make a point."

"Which is?" she asked, warily watching his hands move over her foot.

"That there are plenty of ways to enjoy being around a man without feeling like you're obligated somehow to fall into bed with him. So you can let yourself have a little fun now and then without having to cross any lines you don't want to cross. Do you understand what I'm saying?"

Shannon nodded but kept her gaze on his hands instead of looking directly at him, and her shyness made Michael feel a surge of...what exactly? Protectiveness? He gave her foot a reassuring sort of squeeze and pressed his fingers deeper into the underside of her sole.

It was hardly one of the most intimate things he had ever done with a woman, but somehow the fact he knew this was no small thing for her made it more of a big deal for him, too. He was careful not to let his hands drift any higher than her ankle even though the lines of her calf were sleek and inviting. It was, in fact, the most platonic foot rub he had ever given a woman, and yet his gut seemed to be tightening on him unexpectedly. Maybe he *was* turning into the big bad wolf. "See? Not so bad, is it?" he asked with forced casualness.

She made a sound that was part pleasure and part surprise as he applied deeper pressure, and his gut tightened further. "That actually feels really good," she admitted. "I think you've done this before."

"A few times." He felt the tension in her muscles gradually relax beneath his fingers, and he felt absurdly pleased with himself.

Leaning back in the chair, she placed her other foot on his jean-clad thigh.

Michael started to grin, and he switched feet. "Very subtle."

"I learned it from my dog. Hey, you said we should practice, and I'm trying to be cooperative." She closed her eyes and sighed as his fingers found a small knot of tension. "Yeah, this is…ooo… really not so bad. Can we practice this every day?"

"Quick study, aren't we?"

There was the faintest hint of a smile on her lips. Nice, full lips. With her eyes still closed, he could watch her without making either one of them feel self-conscious.

He liked Shannon Mahoney. There was no doubt about it. From her fiery hair to the tips of her aching toes. It was hard to believe that in a week's time he had gone from wanting to throttle her to offering her a foot massage. But Shannon was an unusual woman. If Drew had half a brain, he would pay her a little more attention.

Michael's fingers slowed in their movements.

Shannon opened her eyes then as if he had signaled the end of the massage. "So, did I pass?"

He let her foot go, startled from his train of thought. "What?"

"Did I shrink?"

"Oh. No. A-plus." He stood up from the bed and ran a hand through his hair. "Foot rubs one day, on to lotions and orgies the next."

"What? No stops in between?"

Lord, but she did make him smile. He reached down to help her up, and she put her hands in his with only the briefest of hesitation. Progress, he thought as he pulled her gently to her feet. "Oh, sweetheart, there are plenty of stops, and I encourage you to explore them all further."

It was a small room, and the close proximity of the bed to the chair meant that Michael's proximity to Shannon was also close. He held her hands for a second longer than he had to, until right before her eyes met his, and then he released them. Now who's shrinking away? he thought, wondering at his behavior, and he stepped to one side to give her more room to get by him.

She slipped her feet back into her shoes, wincing as she did so. "These things are horrible. I don't know if I can make it through another day with them."

"Lose them, then." He kind of liked the way she looked out of them, actually. "Men don't care half as much about shoes as women seem to anyway."

"Yeah, maybe. Besides, another day in heels and I may be too crippled to stand up tomorrow night."

"Something happening tomorrow?"

"Big charity benefit for some of the local youth organizations. A chili cook-off in the park. You haven't seen the flyers around town? Bright orange?"

"Guess my mind was elsewhere."

"Well, part of it is a bachelor auction, and your brother agreed to participate."

The thought of Drew being sold to the highest bidder amused Michael until another thought occurred to him, and then somehow it wasn't as funny anymore. "You planning on bidding?" He should be encouraging her to be bold like that, and didn't understand his reluctance to do so.

"Me?" Her eyes widened. "I don't have the guts or the money, especially after my shopping spree the other day. No, Clarissa insisted we go as a show of support. She and her husband are taking me."

"I doubt she had to twist your arm too hard."

"You'd be surprised," she said under her breath, and he had to strain to hear her.

"What does that mean?"

She shrugged and headed toward the door. "Nothing. Forget it."

"Tell me," he persisted, following her.

Pausing at the door, Shannon put one finger to her temple as if thinking hard. "Let's see. Go to a big party where I get to watch women with more charm, guts, and money than I'll ever have compete with each other to see who gets to walk out of there on Drew's arm. I had my fill of that in high school, thank you very much."

"Oh." None of that had occurred to him. "Well, it doesn't have to be like that."

"Why? Mind over matter?" she said with what he thought might be sarcasm, or possibly a touch of bitterness.

"No. Just…use tomorrow night as an opportunity to practice what we talked about. Forget about Drew for a little while and try flirting with somebody else. Nothing serious, just have a little fun. Truth is, that could work to your advantage anyway. Drew sees you with somebody else, he might start to get a little jealous."

"I don't know. That kind of game-playing reminds me of high school, too," she returned dryly.

"High school is over," he reminded her, remembering the way she described her experiences at McKinley. "Whoever or whatever you thought you were then, you get to decide who you want to be now."

"Easier said than done. Anyway," she said a little too brightly a moment later, "I'll keep you posted about Drew and the youth center, okay?"

Michael stood in the doorway and watched her leave. It was true enough, what he had just told her. But her words "easier said than done" were ones he could relate to, also. The past was a hard thing from which to free yourself.

$$\cdots$$

Shannon got in her truck, kicked off her shoes again, and stared through the windshield. That was not the evening she expected when she decided to come here. It was supposed to be a quick chat, nothing more. How on earth had she wound up with her feet in his lap?

It turned out to be surprisingly nice, though. And not just as a soothing treatment for her aching feet. Truthfully, she was a little sorry when he stopped. He was annoyingly perceptive about her lack of experience with men, and there had been something deliciously decadent about enjoying something so simple as having Michael rub her feet. For a moment there, feeling his hands on her and listening to the sound of his voice as he teased her, she had forgotten there was any sort of arrangement between them, even forgotten that the only reason she was spending time with him was because of Drew.

It was entirely possible, she thought with some confusion, that despite her best intentions she was starting to like Michael Kingston.

Chapter Six

"Well?"

Shannon deliberately kept her eyes on her computer screen. "What?"

"You know perfectly well 'what,'" Clarissa rebuked her. "Your date. How did it go last night?"

"It wasn't really so much a date as..."

"Coffee, drinks, meet-and-greet—whatever you want to call it. Tell me all about this guy of yours. Is he handsome?"

"Um. Yes," Shannon agreed hesitantly, picturing Michael in her head. "Very, actually."

"Smart? Funny? Charming?"

She nodded. He was definitely that.

"For a blind date, this sounds like it was fantastic." Clarissa rubbed her hands together with delight. "So what's his name?"

Please ring, please ring, Shannon thought at her phone, but it didn't oblige her. "He...you know, truthfully, I'd rather not talk a whole lot about him right now, Clarissa. No offense."

"Don't want to jinx anything, is that it? All right, I can take a hint. But just tell me one more thing. Are you going to see him again?"

"I think that's a safe bet."

Her coworker sighed with happiness. "Okay, I'll get out of your hair now. But please humor an old married lady and let me know how things go."

Shannon nodded, helpless to do anything else. This was a fine mess she was creating for herself here. There had to be a good way to nip it in the bud before she wound up with an imaginary husband and a couple of imaginary children.

The phone on her desk suddenly rang, startling her. She gave it a scathing look. "Oh, sure, now you do it," she muttered at it before picking up the receiver. "Drew Kingston's office. Shannon speaking. May I help you?"

"Is Drew available? Tell him it's Lana calling." The voice was breezy and confident. "I'll hold."

"And what may I say this is regarding?"

"It's a personal matter. He'll know." There was an impatient edge to the caller's well-bred voice.

Personal. Shannon knew exactly what that meant. She wondered if "Lana" had enjoyed the dinner reservations at Le Joli the other night and was briefly tempted to *accidentally* hang up on her. "Just a moment, please," she said, and she knew her voice sounded frosty. Putting the woman on hold, she pressed the button for the intercom to Drew's office while she stared at the blinking light on her phone.

His voice answered. "Yes?"

"You have a call on line one. Lana? She says it's—"

"I'll take it. Thanks, Shannon."

After a moment the blinking light turned solid again, and she knew he had picked up. She also had a feeling she knew who was going to be bidding on Drew tonight.

• • •

Forget it. She couldn't take the high heels for one moment longer. It would have to be flats tonight.

Shannon reached into her closet to pull out a pair of plain white sandals and then held them up in the mirror next to one of her new purchases. It was a simple sundress, white and embellished with bits of crocheted lace here and there that gave it a vintage look. It was pretty and feminine, and totally unlike the things she usually bought. The saleslady had picked out everything else, but Shannon had chosen this one. Why, she wasn't sure. Maybe there was a part of her that secretly longed for an occasional dose of frilly girl things to go along with her power tools.

Dressing quickly, she glanced at the clock. She was still on schedule. It must be her nerves that made her feel otherwise. It wasn't really Drew she was nervous about, or even this Lana, who would almost certainly be there tonight. No, she was determined to do as Michael suggested and try to ignore Drew's presence in favor of other men, for this evening anyway. It couldn't really be that hard, not if she jumped right in. A smile here, a joke there… she could learn to flirt. This would be the perfect opportunity to practice.

If only she weren't terrified.

Her hands shook slightly as she wound her hair up into a tight bun and pinned it in place. It was like being sixteen again and going to a school dance. What if no one danced with her? What if the other girls exchanged knowing looks and giggled as she walked past? One could only keep one's chin up and shoulders back for so long before feeling a panicky need to flee.

She was being ridiculous, she told herself firmly. She was not sixteen anymore, and this was a charity benefit, not the prom. People would be there tonight to support a good cause, not reestablish social strata.

Besides, it was too late to come up with a good excuse not to go. She heard the sound of tires on gravel and knew Clarissa and her husband were here.

Funny, but she found herself wishing Michael was coming tonight. It would have been comforting somehow. Her hand hovered over her cell phone momentarily as she felt a fleeting urge to call and invite him. Then she came to her senses and scooped up her phone and keys to drop them into her purse. They were partners, she reminded herself. Not friends.

"Wish me luck," she said to Bo with more cheer than she felt. He wagged his tail and licked her hand before leaping onto her bed and snuggling down into the comforter. "And no wild parties while I'm gone, young man, you hear?"

He started to snore softly.

When Shannon stepped out onto the porch, Clarissa gave her a quick hug. "Shannon, you remember Jeff, right?"

"Yes, of course," Shannon said politely to the middle-aged man fiddling with his tie as he stood beside his wife. "Christmas party, right?"

"Yep. I was Santa." He patted his generous stomach unselfconsciously and grinned. "Can't imagine why, huh?"

"Dear," Clarissa said to Shannon, "you look lovely, but there's something I just have to do. Please forgive me."

"What do you—hey!" Shannon's mouth fell open as the older woman abruptly pulled the hairpins from Shannon's hair and sent it tumbling down around her shoulders.

"There. Much better," Clarissa said smugly, carefully arranging fiery orange waves.

"What are you doing?" She tried to wind her hair back up again, but Clarissa stubbornly refused to hand over the hairpins and instead stuffed them into her purse.

"Honey, so help me, if you try to put that beautiful hair of yours back into a bun or a braid or even a ponytail, you'll be riding to town in the trunk of the car instead of the back seat. Leave it down, trust me."

"I can't wear it down! Someone's liable to throw water on me because they think my head's on fire. Seriously, Clarissa—"

Her friend gently took Shannon's hands in hers. "Shannon, I don't know when or why you ever decided your hair was unsightly somehow, but it's not. It's full of vibrancy and color, and you shouldn't try to hide it from the rest of the world."

To her shock, Shannon's eyes were suddenly wet. How could a few kind words be enough to make her cry? Especially after a childhood full of unkind ones should have hardened her long ago. "I'm sorry," she said with a shaky laugh as she quickly wiped her eyes. "This is silly. I don't know what's wrong with me. I'm having flashbacks to school days, I guess. Don't mind me." Carrot-top was one of the gentler things kids had said about her then.

Clarissa cupped her cheek for a moment and then gave her another hug. "Come on. Let's go before all the good parking spots are gone and we have to walk five miles to even *see* the park. And I mean it, leave the hair down or I will have Jeff lock you in the car. He does what I tell him to, you know."

"It's true," Jeff agreed, frowning at an ink stain on his tie and wiping at it uselessly. Shannon laughed weakly but obediently left her hair alone as she followed them to their car.

• • •

Michael turned off the television after going through all the channels without really seeing any of them. He crossed the tiny motel room for about the tenth time in the last twenty minutes and stared out the window at his so-called view, restless as a caged animal. He could always take a drive into town and play a game of pool, maybe pick up a pretty girl and make a night of it …

But somehow that held about as little interest for him as the television. He pulled the orange flyer he'd picked up from an earlier errand from his back pocket and read it again. Shannon was right; these things were like traffic cones. How had he ever missed them? Because he'd had too many other things on his mind, he supposed.

He glanced over the events listed on the flyer, considering his options. Well, he did like chili, after all. There would be music, dancing, and lots of folks having a good time. What's not to like? he thought. Maybe he would even get a chance to see how Shannon was doing with the "homework" he'd given her. See if she was having a good time with some new guy.

Just as long as she wasn't having too much fun. He pictured her clinging a little too closely to a man on the dance floor, and it made him frown.

It shouldn't bother him. It was her business after all, and even though she was inexperienced, she was hardly a child. Then again, he reminded himself, there were some guys out there who wouldn't hesitate to take advantage of her naiveté around men. It was a mentor's job to look out for his protégé, wasn't it? He owed it to her to make sure she was okay. It was the ethical and responsible thing to do.

Oh, yes, and his brother would be there. He had almost forgotten that. Maybe he would run into him, too.

All right then, it looked like he was going out. Peeling off his T-shirt, Michael headed for the shower to make himself presentable for polite society.

•••

It was a good turnout, Shannon thought, keeping a careful distance between her white dress and anyone carrying a bowl of chili. Between the food and the bachelor auction, it seemed likely they'd raise a respectable sum of money tonight for charity. She left Clarissa and Jeff to dance with each other on the temporary dance floor that had been set up near the band, smiling at the sight of the stout middle-aged man dipping his wife with surprising grace.

Congratulating herself on her decision to wear the comfortable sandals tonight, she walked across the grass and through the crowd of jovial attendees. Her first instinct was to hide out off to the side somewhere, preferably in the shadows, but she forced herself to get out in the thick of things, nodding and smiling at people she passed.

It seemed so easy for everybody else. Why was it so hard for her? She was probably overthinking it, she decided, self-consciously tucking a wayward lock of hair behind one ear. She should be casual and natural, just go with the flow and see where it took her.

There, for example. Right by the edge of the stage where the bachelor auction would be starting soon. A man in a blue blazer and khaki pants stood by himself, scanning the crowd with his eyes and sipping something from a paper cup. He looked non-threatening and reasonably attractive, too. Why not just strike up a conversation with him?

"Hi," she greeted him cheerfully, coming to a stop near him. "Having a good time?"

"What? Oh, sure," he said, obviously distracted and not really seeing her. "Listen, do you know where the restrooms are around here? That chili packed a real punch, and I gotta hit the head in a real bad way, if you know what I mean."

Taken slightly aback, she pointed the way for him and he left, taking long, desperate strides.

Not exactly what she expected, but at least she had made the effort. She heard the sound of someone tapping on a microphone then, and looked up to see the evening's MC, a silver-haired radio personality, take center stage. "Ladies and gentlemen, I want to thank you all for coming out tonight to support some real worthwhile foundations in our fair city. The evening's main event is about to begin, so ladies, grab your checkbooks and get ready to start some bidding wars. Could I have all of the bachelors backstage now, please?"

As a crowd began to gather in front of the stage, Shannon glanced to the side and spotted Drew. He was heading for the stage as directed, and on his arm was a woman who she presumed must be Lana. She was tall and willowy, dark-haired, and impeccably dressed. She also, Shannon noticed, had absolutely no trouble walking in high heels. Laughing at something Drew said, she turned his face toward hers with long and flawlessly manicured nails and gave him a light kiss on the cheek. It felt a bit like watching a traffic accident. She wanted to turn away, but she couldn't, not even when Drew looked over and spotted her.

In her head, she thought a very bad word. Outwardly, she smiled brightly and waved.

To her dismay, he led his date over to her and made introductions. "Shannon, glad you could come out tonight. Lana Akers, this is Shannon Mahoney, my assistant. Shannon, this is Lana."

She kept her smile plastered onto her face. "Very nice to meet you."

"You, too," Lana returned, smiling politely but indifferently.

Neither woman extended her hand, but Drew didn't seem to notice. "Well, I'd better get backstage. Wish me luck."

"You don't need luck," Lana told him with a coquettish wink, and Shannon tried not to roll her eyes. "You've got me. I promise you won't get stuck with any nightmarish bidders, okay? Now, go on before they bump you from the list."

He waved goodbye and disappeared somewhere behind the stage, leaving the two women alone together.

There was no help for it. She was going to have to make polite conversation with the woman. "So," Shannon began, "what do you do for a living, Lana?"

"What? Oh, I do financial advising. Stocks, annuities, portfolios…I'm sure you'd find it all a bit dry," she answered absently, her eyes busy searching the crowd.

Translation: I'm not smart enough to understand it. And yet phrased with barely a hint of condescension. Ms. Akers was very good at this. "And where did you meet Drew?"

"At the country club. We're both members. I don't think I've seen you there, have I?" Without waiting for a response, Lana put a hand up suddenly and signaled someone else in the crowd. "Elizabeth! Over here!"

A shapely blonde who was every bit Lana's equal in style and stature made her way over to them. "Lana! I should have known you'd be up front."

"Absolutely. Drew's going home with me tonight, and I'm not taking any chances otherwise. Oh, Elizabeth, this is Drew's assistant—I'm sorry, what was your name again?"

"Shannon." It was not that hard a name to remember.

"Right. Would you excuse me for just a second, Elizabeth?" Lana bent her head so that she could lean closer to Shannon's ear. "Let's be very clear with each other, all right, Shannon? I'm a very aggressive woman, and when I see something I want, I go after it until it's mine."

Shannon drew back and frowned at her. "Your point being?"

"Drew. I know when another woman wants the man I want. Drew may not realize it, but I do. If you think you have the advantage because you work for him, don't kid yourself. You're out of your league here."

Speechless, Shannon could only stare at her as heat flooded her cheeks.

"So don't even think about making a play for him, because you will only wind up embarrassing yourself." Lana straightened and turned back to Elizabeth, effectively dismissing Shannon. "I think we understand each other."

• • •

From atop a grassy knoll in the park, Michael spotted Shannon standing near the stage. The crowd was too noisy for him to hear the MC very well, but he caught enough of his announcements to understand the bachelor auction was about to get underway. He should have known he would find Shannon near wherever Drew was going to be.

It was her hair that caught his attention first, even in the dwindling twilight. Finally free of any fetters, it fell over her shoulders like cascading fire, and the effect of it made his pulse quicken unexpectedly. She stood out from the rest of the crowd like a brilliant jewel in a pile of ordinary rubble, and the wonder of all wonders was how the people standing around her didn't seem to see it.

He saw a dark-haired woman lean in to say something to Shannon, and then watched as Shannon's face burned with embarrassment. His jaw twitched, and he frowned.

Girls can be catty. Wasn't that what she had said before?

The brunette turned her back on Shannon, as if she were second-hand news, leaving Shannon to try and recover from the obvious snub.

Oh, hell no, he thought. Not on his watch.

And Michael began to push his way through the sea of people.

• • •

It was like high school all over again. Shannon struggled to think of something to say, something clever or biting, but her mind drew an absolute blank. The shock of having her feelings exposed aloud and then essentially stomped beneath the stylish heel of a rival who clearly found her to be no threat at all left her feeling dizzy and shaken.

The MC was saying something, and the crowd was starting to cheer, but Shannon didn't hear much of anything except for a roaring sound in her ears.

Part of her wanted to slink away and hide. Another part of her wanted to tap Lana Akers on the shoulder and then deck her.

Before she could recover enough to come up with a third and more socially acceptable option, the crowd nearby parted to let someone pass, and her eyes widened at the sight of Michael appearing suddenly a few yards in front of her. His black T-shirt and jeans were nothing fancy, but somehow on him they made every other man within a ten-mile radius seem underdressed, and most of the women who had gathered around for the auction stared at him instead of at the stage.

"Please tell me we can bid on *him*," someone murmured appreciatively from nearby.

A heart-stopping smile made his perfect mouth curve slowly upward, and his eyes never left Shannon's as he made his way between a stunned Lana and Elizabeth to reach her. "Hello, sweetheart," he said in a voice that could have melted chocolate, completely ignoring the other women. He twined her fingers in his for a moment and then slid his hands up her arms to cup her face, sending a jolt of unexpected fire through her body. "Sorry I'm late. Parking was insane."

And then he pulled her in closer to put those sinful lips of his on hers.

Chapter Seven

Shannon stiffened in shock, but her shock slowly melted into something else. Or maybe she melted into Michael. All she really knew was that his hands found their way to her hips, which made it feel like the most natural thing in the world to let her arms slide up over his shoulders and around his neck in return.

His hands tightened gently around her waist, pulling her closer to him, and she went very willingly. Dear God, he was good at this. Granted, she didn't have much to compare it with, but surely most men weren't able to do the things he was able to with just his mouth. It couldn't be natural for a man to fill a woman with fire like this within the space of about three seconds.

Somewhere in the back of her mind, she recalled the knowing looks girls in school had exchanged when they talked about Michael Kingston. Now she understood what it was all about.

The sounds of the auction slowly brought her back to awareness, and she rather dazedly separated her lips from his.

"So, anyway, that's why I'm late," Michael said easily, as if such kisses happened all the time. Maybe they did for him. Heedless of who might be watching, he traced her mouth with his finger and smiled that wicked smile of his. "Promise I'll make it up to you later, though."

Her heart pounded. Oh, yes. He was very good at this.

She didn't dare look him in the eye for fear he would see just how out of her element she really felt at that moment. To her embarrassment, her knees were unsteady and about to give out. She willed them to stiffen and turned her eyes away from Michael's face to look over his shoulder. That was when she saw Lana's jaw practically on the ground.

And, right or wrong, that gave her a delicious feeling of satisfaction.

He had seen it, she realized suddenly. The snub. And he had kissed her to help her stick it to Lana. It was wrong of her to be pleased by that, she was sure, but she couldn't bring herself to be sorry just yet. Maybe tomorrow. Or maybe in fifty years.

"Checking out my competition?" Michael gave a quick nod in the direction of the stage. "Not thinking of replacing me, I hope?"

She finally found her voice, but it wavered slightly as she tried to form a coherent response. "Uh, no. No, of course not."

"Good. Let's keep it that way." He put an arm around her shoulders, a sideways embrace that felt warm and natural. "If it's all the same to you, though, I'd like to remove you from temptation's path. Why don't you say good night to your friends and let me take you home?"

"What? Oh. Good night, Lana." She started to turn away and then froze as she realized Drew was the bachelor up for auction onstage, and his attention was most definitely on the two of them.

Shannon felt sudden tension in Michael's arm and knew he had just realized it, too. His brother wore a poorly disguised look of shock on his face, and were it not for the fact he was in a very public place, Shannon had a feeling he had a few choice words to say to Michael.

Well, she wanted to get his attention. It looked like she succeeded. She had mixed feelings about that.

"Sold! To the lovely lady in red. You can pay for your bachelor at that table to the left of the stage, ma'am. Our next bachelor..."

Beside them, Lana did a double take as she realized she had missed the bidding on Drew. A gleeful gray-haired socialite blew him a kiss instead as she made her way up to the table to write out a check. Had her mouth not suddenly gone dry when she realized

Drew had witnessed her kiss his brother, Shannon might have enjoyed the look on Lana's face a little more. As it was, she felt like squirming under his gaze.

"Let's get out of here before he comes down from that stage," Michael murmured into her ear, and she willingly let him lead her away through the crowd, wondering what on earth she was going to say when she saw Drew the next morning.

Halfway across the park, Shannon hesitated when she saw an openmouthed Clarissa staring at the two of them from the edge of the dance floor. Oh, boy, was Shannon going to have a lot of explaining to do tomorrow. She made a furtive gesture to indicate she was leaving with Michael and then quickly looked away before her friend could protest.

Michael led her to his truck. "Care for a drive?" he asked as if nothing unusual had just happened. He opened the passenger's side door for her.

"Where are we going?" she asked tersely, her voice sounding choked even to her.

"Don't know yet. Someplace where my brother isn't."

She glanced back at the noise and lights of the fundraiser.

"You can stay if you want."

His voice was neutral, and she couldn't tell what he was feeling besides the urge to get out of there. "No," she said, still feeling lightheaded after kissing him, even if it was only for show. "I don't think I'm quite ready to face questions yet."

"Climb in, then."

She did, her pulse racing quite a bit faster than usual, and this time it had nothing to do with Drew. She watched Michael walk around the front of his truck after he closed her door for her, wondering at how unaffected he seemed by what had happened. If he was concerned about Drew's reaction to seeing them together, he didn't show it beyond a single glance back over his shoulder in the direction of the stage. And if he were at all self-conscious about kissing Shannon, there was absolutely no sign of that in his demeanor either.

All right. She would play it cool then, too. Well, she would try, at least. So the man was a good kisser. It shouldn't exactly come as a shock to her, given his long-standing reputation with women. And she had enjoyed it. Well, that was only natural, too, when one's partner was so good at it. Inexperienced bumpkin that she was, even she knew a kiss was only a kiss. It didn't mean anything.

Except that he had come to her rescue during a painfully awkward situation. She had not expected anything like that from him. "Why did you do that?" she asked him as he got into the truck, wishing the words didn't sound so awkward and stiff.

"You mean back there?" Michael put the key in the ignition and started the engine. "Sorry if I caught you off guard. I was just trying to help."

Off guard was an understatement. "Yeah, I figured, but…" She stared at him, and she knew the rest of her question was written all over her face. *Why would you care?*

He looked at her, his gaze dropping momentarily to her mouth, and she knew she blushed yet again. So much for playing it cool. "I don't like snobs," he said finally, and he put the truck in reverse.

•••

Without consciously planning it, Michael drove to the football field at McKinley High School. This time of day, with darkness falling and evening well underway, the school was long-deserted and empty. "I haven't been back here in years," he said, looking the old building over through his windshield. "Have you?"

"No," Shannon said very softly from beside him.

He glanced over at her. She had barely said two words since leaving the park—and the kiss—behind them. He didn't think she was offended by his actions. Startled, maybe, but not offended. It was clear to him the moment his lips met hers that she was as inexperienced in the area of kissing as she was in everything else that had to do with the opposite sex, but there was something indescribably sweet about that to him. And, anyway, she was a quick study.

Right now she was studying their old campus with a very solemn expression on her face. Wary, even. She must have had at least one or two fond memories of high school, but if so, she didn't seem to be remembering them now.

Michael glanced up through the glass of the windshield at the stars that were coming out. "Did you ever go to the football games here?"

"Me?" she returned, surprised. "No."

"How about the victory parties?"

Shannon shook her head with a wry smile. "I heard those things could get pretty wild."

"Yeah, they could. That was kind of the point. A little wild oat sowing to celebrate things."

"Why do I have a feeling you sowed more than a little?"

"Guilty as charged." Michael opened the driver's side door. "Come on."

"Where are we going?"

"Just getting a better view." He got out and went up to sit on the hood of the truck. High school was not a time in his life he would really care to go back to, but there were times when he wished he could do a few things over. Just a few small changes, and he wondered if his life could have gone very differently.

Michael heard the sound of the passenger's side door opening, and he turned his head to see Shannon emerge tentatively from the truck. He patted the space next to him on the hood in invitation.

She shook her head. "That's okay. I'll stand."

"Shannon?"

"What?"

"You're shrinking again."

She opened her mouth as if to protest, but seemed to think better of it. "I *can't* sit there."

"Why not?"

In answer, she glanced pointedly down at her clean white dress.

"Oh. Right. Just a second." A few moments later, Michael pulled his leather jacket from the truck and spread it out over the hood. "There. No excuses now, right?"

Wordlessly, she settled carefully next to him, not quite close enough to touch, and turned her face toward the stars rather than the field.

"So, no football, no parties…what did you do in high school?"

"Studied. Kept to myself, mostly."

"Because of catty girls?"

"Maybe."

He waited for her to explain, but she remained quiet. "Maybe?" he prompted finally. "What did they give you a hard time about?"

Shannon ticked reasons off of her fingers one by one. "I didn't wear the right kind of clothes, I didn't come from the right side of town, my hair looked like a Halloween decoration—"

"Your hair is beautiful."

She grew quiet again. Self-conscious? Partly, he realized, but that wasn't completely the reason. She was also trying to figure out what to do with his compliment. He wasn't sure what to do with it, either, so he changed the subject. "Forget education. High school is all about status. Always was and always will be. Everybody wants to climb higher on the social ladder, and some people figure they can only do that by stepping on somebody else. None of it means anything, not really."

"Spoken like someone who was snugly at the top of said social ladder."

"If I was at the top, it was purely by accident. Hell, I didn't even want to be on the ladder in the first place."

"No? Seemed like you enjoyed a *little* of the attention."

He laughed humorlessly. "You mean, because girls chased me? Yeah, sure. It's just too bad they were chasing me for all the wrong reasons."

"What do you mean?"

"Status, sweetheart, status. They liked what they thought I could give them, they didn't care about *me*."

"How can you be so sure?"

"Experience."

"Come on. You really think there couldn't have been at least one girl who really and truly liked the real you?"

"No one in high school *knew* the real me." He wasn't sure if anyone had since then, either.

She played with the hem of her dress absently, considering his words. "Sounds a little cynical," she said finally, without looking at him.

"Cynical? Me? I'm the poster child for optimism."

The only response she gave him was a noncommittal sort of sound. "Sometimes I wonder…"

"Wonder what?"

"I wonder if anybody ever really gets over high school."

"I hope so."

"Me, too."

Lying back against the windshield to get comfortable, Michael put his hands behind his head and studied her. Maybe it was the starlight, or maybe it was the fact her hair was down for once… or maybe it was because she was still self-conscious about him kissing her, but there was something different about her manner. Something softer. He enjoyed her sarcasm, but he liked this, too. He reached out to run a few strands of her hair through his fingers, so lightly that he knew she was unaware he did it.

"So what do you think Drew will say tomorrow?" she asked, clearing her throat with her face still turned upward.

He let her hair slip free from his hand. "To me or to you?"

"Both, I guess."

"He'll want to kick my butt from here to kingdom come, I imagine. And you he'll want to caution against getting involved with an SOB like me, or something to that effect. Actually, the whole thing could work to your advantage. Now he gets to swoop in and be your protector."

"Probably didn't help your cause any, though, did it?"

That thought had crossed his mind, too. "Can't be helped now."

"I'm sorry."

Michael shrugged it off. "Not your fault. I was the one who kissed you, not the other way around." He kept his voice casual, but inwardly he was anxious. "Hopefully you can still get him to listen."

"I'll try." She hesitated. "I didn't expect to see you there tonight."

"I didn't expect to go."

She finally turned her head to look at him. "What changed your mind?"

The truth was that he wasn't really sure, so he spoke flippantly. "I'm just an impulsive kind of guy. If Drew hasn't mentioned that to you already, I'm sure it'll be on the top of his to-do list now."

Several minutes passed before Shannon spoke again "Michael?"

It was the first time he could remember her addressing him by name. "Yes?"

"Will you tell me why your family's home is so important to you?"

The change in subjects caught him off guard. "I already told you."

"No, I mean really."

For a moment he considered continuing to deny that there was anything more. He thought she would help him regardless, especially after tonight, but she would be disappointed in him. That possibility did not appeal to him at all. Against all odds, they seemed to be becoming friends, and he was reluctant to risk messing that up now. "I screwed up. Now I'm trying to fix things," he said finally.

"What do you mean?"

He stared at the night sky, thinking back to his years with his family and feeling the shame that always went with those memories now. "I was a troublesome little punk as a kid—well, you may remember some of that firsthand. Chip on my shoulder the size of a house and always looking for trouble."

"I remember."

"I caused a lot of trouble for my parents back then. A lot of heartache. There's a lot I wish I could take back."

"Lots of teenagers make life difficult for their parents."

"Yeah, but then they have time to apologize. I blew that." He cleared his throat. "There was a car accident a few years ago. Took both my parents."

"I remember that, too," she said softly.

"Yeah, I guess it did make all the papers."

"So you're doing this for them?"

"That home meant a lot to my parents. Protecting it's the last thing I can do for them." He could feel her watching him in the dark, waiting for him to explain further, but he didn't feel up to it. "So there you have it. Man, I was quite the bad seed in high school, wasn't I?" he added more lightly, veering away from painful memories and praying she would let him.

She did, for which he was grateful. "Kind of. I don't remember a whole lot, though. My focus was more on your brother."

Drew again. He felt a flicker of jealousy that shouldn't have been there.

"But I remember the way all the girls mooned over you, of course. And I remember that you got in a lot of fights."

"Self-defense, I swear. I had a lot of angry boyfriends coming after me at the time."

"Did you ever consider not making out with their girlfriends?"

"I was a horny teenage boy. That was not an option." She gave an incredulous little laugh, and he liked the sound. "Half the time girls just made stuff up anyway about what happened to get attention, so I figured as long as I was going to get in trouble for it, I might as well enjoy it."

"I suppose that's one approach," she returned dryly.

"Uh, oh. You disapprove, don't you?"

"Do you care?"

More than she might have guessed. "Well, I don't steal girlfriends anymore."

"Reformed, huh?"

"More like 'recovering.'"

"Ah. On the wagon. Is there a twelve-step program for that kind of thing?"

"No. I'm on my own." Funny how words said so lightly could suddenly feel so heavy. They hung there in the air, and even if Shannon didn't notice any change in Michael's demeanor, he felt a subtle shift in his mood.

But maybe she did notice, because he felt the fingers of her hand brush against his ever so lightly as if she wanted to give his hand a comforting squeeze but wasn't bold enough to do so. He curled his hand around hers instead, wondering if she would pull away. She didn't.

"Michael?" she said after a minute.

"Yes?"

"I'll talk to Drew again about the youth center. I promise."

He ran his thumb across hers. Her skin was warm and soft, and it occurred to him that it would be so easy right now to pull her just a little bit closer. And from there it wouldn't take much to turn her face to his. Kisses had always been such casual things for him. Light. Fun. There was no reason to think that kissing Shannon wouldn't also be fun, especially after the taste he'd gotten of it in the park. But something told him there would be nothing light about it.

This was crazy, and he almost laughed out loud at himself. Weighing the pros and cons of kissing Shannon Mahoney right here, right now on the hood of his truck. What was he thinking? It must be some sort of mojo about the place, or maybe memories of making out with beautiful girls years ago at the football field that were putting wild ideas into his head. He liked Shannon, that was all. She made him laugh. She made him think about something else besides past mistakes. It didn't mean he wanted her.

Besides, she wanted his brother.

And yet, his eyes focused on the silhouette of her mouth anyway.

She nudged him then, and he quickly looked away before she could catch him staring at her lips. "Hey, look, Coach," she said softly in what he knew was an attempt to lighten the mood a little as she held up their joined hands between them. "No shrinking. Proud of me?"

He squeezed her hand and spoke with more lightness than he felt. "Very." In spite of his attempt to be rational about the whole thing, Michael realized something that disconcerted him.

Sitting beside this woman who dreamed of being with Drew, he envied his brother.

• • •

Shannon left her hand in Michael's. He seemed to be in no hurry to take his hand back, so she told herself there was no reason for her to take hers back, either. Had he noticed the way her breath caught when he first touched her? She hoped not. She wasn't used to holding a man's hand, that was all, and it was a little embarrassing to have her inexperience constantly shine through. Now that she was over her initial startle, she admitted to herself that she liked the way it felt to have her fingers wrapped in his. He did it so easily, too, she knew he couldn't be as turned around by it as she was.

Everything seemed to come so naturally to Michael. She had heard a heaviness in his words and felt an impulse to say or do something to let him know that he wasn't quite as alone as he thought he was, but then lost her nerve. He, on the other hand, showed no hesitation at all in taking her hand. Did he ever second-guess himself? Well, apparently he did when it came to his parents. She hadn't missed the way he steered conversation away from them as soon as possible.

And despite the way he used humor to try to cover the fact, she had a sneaking suspicion about something else. Michael Kingston didn't like himself very much. And yet, oddly enough, she was liking him more and more.

She had no illusions that the kiss in the park had been anything more than for show, but her mouth still tingled at the memory of it. She nearly touched her lips with her free hand but stopped herself just in time. Michael already thought she was naïve and inexperienced as it was. There was no need to prove him right any further tonight. One kiss, and he had her head all mixed up. She was attracted to Drew, not Michael, she reminded herself.

After a long while, he squeezed her hand again, sending a tremor down her spine. "Come on. I'll take you home."

The ride home was long and quiet. Shannon wanted to say something about the way he had come to her aid in the park with that kiss, but she couldn't think of anything appropriately casual enough. Something easy and airy that would let him know she understood the true nature of what lay behind it—something that would prove she was worldly enough to know better than to keep thinking about it. Honestly she was.

Nothing. Her mind drew a complete blank.

Funny, but even though the kiss was the thing that had most knocked her off her feet at the time, it was the hand-holding in the school parking lot that left her the most bemused. Maybe because, innocent as it was, there was nothing about it that had been for show. She shouldn't make more out of it than it was, but the problem was she didn't know for sure what *it* was to begin with.

Shannon glanced over at Michael. His attention appeared to be solely on the road, and if he was thinking at all about the same things she was, he gave no sign of it. There might have been a vaguely distracted air about him, but she might just as easily have imagined it. More likely, he was thinking about the future of his parents' home and Drew's possible reaction to what had happened tonight.

He pulled the truck into her driveway and came to a stop in front of her house. "Home sweet home."

It might be wiser to simply say good night and go inside, but she hesitated, wanting to say something that would let him know...what, exactly? Something had changed tonight, even if she wasn't sure what it was or what it meant. "I'm glad you came out tonight," she said, thinking the words a little lame and insufficient even as she said them.

"Me, too."

Stepping out of the truck and shutting the door behind her, she put her face to the open window and allowed herself to give in to a sudden impulse. "Michael?"

"Yeah?"

"I think..."

He waited expectantly for her to finish but didn't try to hurry her.

She said it before she could change her mind. "I think maybe the real you is a better guy than you think."

Her words clearly caught him by surprise, and some unidentifiable emotion flickered into his eyes before he could stop it.

"Well…good night." Shannon turned to go up her front steps before he could speak or she could blurt out anything else she might later regret. She heard the truck idle a few moments longer before Michael finally put it back into drive and headed back down her driveway.

What was that? she asked herself, locking her front door behind her and leaning against it with one hand on her forehead.

Later, in her bed for the night, Shannon stared at the ceiling in the darkness of her room. It was quiet except for the sound of Bo's gentle snores, but she still couldn't sleep. There was Drew to face tomorrow, and Clarissa, but they were not the ones keeping her awake.

No, in the end, that was Michael.

Chapter Eight

The rational part of Shannon's mind told her that staying home from work was not an option. She would have to face the music sooner or later. She also knew that coming in early enough to get to her desk before Clarissa arrived would hardly prevent the older woman from tracking her down, but some part of Shannon must have still believed it possible because she got to work a full thirty minutes before her usual time. Turning on her computer, she put an expression of such focus and concentration on her face, hopefully the other woman would be reluctant to interrupt her. She heard the squeak of the outer doors opening, and she redoubled her efforts to look preoccupied. Who knew? It might grant her a temporary reprieve.

"Ahem."

Then again, maybe not. Shannon sighed inwardly and grudgingly looked up from her work. "Yes?"

Clarissa stood in the doorway, her arms folded across her chest, and Shannon wondered fleetingly if this was how it felt to be caught out past one's curfew. "You're dating Drew's *brother*?"

"Uh..."

"The last time I saw the two of you together, I thought there might be bloodshed. What on earth happened?"

"Well, we—"

"And did you or did you not say he had a bad reputation?"

"In high school, yes, but—"

Clarissa frowned and shook her head warningly. "Shannon, I know he's a very handsome man, and it's easy to be dazzled by that, but you need to use your head here. You're not exactly a woman of the world, and a man like him could easily sweet-talk you into something you might regret later. I'm sure he seems exciting and wonderful now, but—"

"Clarissa!" Heat flooded Shannon's face. "We're just spending a little time together, that's all."

"Really? Because I heard the two of you got pretty hot and heavy at the auction last night."

"Hot and heavy? It was one kiss! I—Look," Shannon said, realizing just how defensive she sounded and struggling to keep her voice calm. "I know you're just looking out for me, and I appreciate it, Clarissa. Really, I do. But even though it may seem on the surface like I'm going off the deep end, please trust me. I know what I'm doing."

"Are you sure? The whole bad boy thing aside, is it a good idea to get involved with your boss's brother? Especially when there's bad blood between the two of them? Oh, Shannon, please think this whole thing through before you take it any further."

"All right, I will," Shannon agreed, desperately hoping this particular conversation would end quickly. "I promise. Okay?"

Her promise must not have been that convincing, because Clarissa continued to frown worriedly at her. "I just don't want to see you get hurt, honey. Please be careful."

Shannon nodded, and Clarissa turned to go to her own desk, still looking unhappy. Guilt flickered to life inside Shannon. Would Clarissa be less worried if she knew the truth about Shannon's arrangement with Michael, or would she fret even more? This was not the way things were supposed to go. It was like planning what was supposed to be a nice little swim in the ocean but then realizing she had wandered too far out past the shallows, and now the currents around her were picking up speed.

The phone rang, and Shannon automatically reached for it even though her head was not at its clearest. She drew a blank for a moment before habit took over and the words spilled out of her mouth. "Drew Kingston's office, Shannon speaking. How may I help you? I'm sorry, he's not in yet, but—" Then someone cleared his throat, and Shannon looked up to see that Drew had taken Clarissa's place in the doorway. His expression was impossible for her to read because it was one she had never seen on his face before. Her mouth went dry, but not in the way it usually did when she saw him. She swallowed and forced herself to speak. "Let me put you on hold for a minute, please." Pressing the appropriate button, she put the receiver back in its place.

"Shannon."

"Good morning," she offered, doing her best to look him in the eye calmly but not finding it easy.

"Shannon, I think we should talk." Drew took a deep breath, as if maybe this wasn't the most comfortable situation for him, either. "About Michael."

She nodded, putting her hands in her lap and clasping her fingers tightly together out of his line of vision. Her entire drive to work had been spent mentally rehearsing for this conversation, but nothing she practiced came to mind now. Better to let him say his piece first, and then maybe inspiration would strike her.

"I realize your personal life is your own business, and who you spend your time with after hours is your choice, but..." Drew ran one hand through his hair, a move that usually made her heart flutter. Today she barely noticed, maybe because her pulse was already faster than usual. "If it were any other man, I'd keep my mouth shut, but because it's Michael, I feel a certain responsibility to speak up. You understand what I mean?"

"I understand."

Drew took a step closer. "It's just that he—"

The phone rang again, and Shannon glanced at the light already blinking from the caller on hold, then she looked back at Drew.

He sighed in obvious frustration. "This isn't the best time and place to do this, is it? All right, my last meeting this morning is over around noon. Can we have lunch together then and talk? I really think we need to."

"Okay, noon. You've got a call waiting on line one," Shannon told him as she reached for the phone, her anxiety making her tone crisper than usual. "Drew Kingston's office. How may I help you?"

Drew moved past her into his office, his jaw tight with tension. As he closed the door behind him, Shannon sank heavily back into her chair and closed her eyes.

• • •

Shannon had no appetite to speak of, but the waiter watched her expectantly, and she finally ordered the soup of the day—whatever it was—just to get him to leave. She really didn't care what he brought her so long as it gave her an excuse not to talk.

She could feel Drew's eyes on her and realized he was about as happy as she was to be having this conversation. Forcing herself to look up, she saw him fingering his tie as if it were too tight.

"I don't quite know where to begin," Drew admitted finally, "but I have to say I was not expecting to see you and Michael together last night." He shook his head in disbelief. "That's the understatement of the year. The two of you—it's the last thing in the world I would have predicted."

Shannon blinked.

"I meant no offense," he said hastily, catching the look on her face. "It's just that you're a nice girl, Shannon, and 'nice' isn't really Michael's type. Which is why I'm so concerned. Michael has always been a bit of a heartbreaker, and I don't want to see you get hurt. So at the risk of crossing the line between professional and personal, I'm going to ask you to reconsider getting involved with him."

Shannon was silent. Here she was, sitting across the table from Drew in a nice restaurant, having lunch with him. This was something she had dreamed about doing for years. Shouldn't she be more excited? Granted, she never imagined it under quite these circumstances, but here she was, the complete focus of his full attention.

It was not as thrilling as she dreamed.

"Please trust me when I say no good can come of it. Michael's main concern is what feels good to Michael. Relationships with women are all about fun for him. Once the newness wears off, he loses interest."

These were all words she expected. They were not so different from things she had thought about Michael herself. But they no longer rang as true as they used to. "I know about Michael's history with women."

"Somehow I doubt he told you everything."

"He didn't have to. I remember him in high school."

"You remember...?" Drew trailed off, momentarily confused as he absorbed her words. "You went to McKinley?"

She nodded. "Same year as you."

Drew looked startled and then a little embarrassed. He began fidgeting with his tie again. "Oh."

This was definitely not how she daydreamed about spending time with him. It was awkward to say the least. The only positive thing she could see about it was that he seemed concerned for her welfare—in a generic sort of way. She struggled to find the right thing to say, but despite her hopes, inspiration refused to come. Honesty would have to do. Well, maybe selective honesty. "Last night with Michael and me..." She paused, her cheeks growing warm. "It wasn't exactly what it looked like. We're spending a little time together is all. You really don't need to worry about me."

"Spending a little time together," Drew repeated, frowning. "Yes."

The look on his face suggested Drew was no more convinced than Clarissa was. "I can't help but think it's a mistake for you to spend any time around him at all. I'd hate to see you do something you'll regret later."

"I appreciate your concern." And she did. It was just too bad that he came across as a stern fatherly type and not as a jealous, red-blooded male. Strangely enough, she felt more irritation than disappointment. It was nice to know people like Drew and Clarissa cared enough to speak up, but did everyone around her really believe she was a naïve idiot? "I'm really okay, though."

"I realize it may seem that way now, but you're too close to the situation to see things clearly. I've seen it before. Michael can have a powerful effect on women, sometimes with disastrous results. Their judgment gets clouded."

"My judgment is fine."

"You may think that, but I'm not sure you're really seeing Michael for who he is," Drew persisted.

He sounded like a broken record, and it was starting to get on her nerves. "You two don't exactly spend a lot of time together, though. Don't you think it's possible he might not be the same person you remember?" She caught her fingers playing nervously with the edge of her napkin and quickly smoothed it back down. Here she was, finally alone with her high school hero, and she was contradicting him. It was hardly one of her romantic fantasies. She swallowed and continued. "People can change."

Dismay flickered over Drew's face, and Shannon realized her words only further convinced him she was under Michael's spell. "See? He's got your head turned around already. He's the misunderstood and long-suffering bad boy, and you're the only one who 'gets' him. Please don't fall for it, Shannon."

She sighed, feeling an unexpected wave of frustration toward him. It made her tongue a little looser than usual. "I'm not falling for anything. The truth is—" She hesitated, debating how much of the truth to reveal to him now. He was too convinced his brother was bad news to keep an open mind about anything that had to do with Michael, and that included the youth center. "Well, the truth is, we've mostly just been talking. You know, about old times. Family, high school, things like that."

"Old times." Drew sounded skeptical.

"Yes. Maybe you should try talking to him. See for yourself if anything's changed."

"Michael and I have nothing to talk about."

"Are you sure?"

"I'm sure."

It was now or never. She took a deep breath and plunged ahead. "How about your parents?"

He stiffened, and she knew she was treading on dangerous ground here. But if she hesitated, she would never have the guts to get the rest of the words out. She told herself it was in his best interest to hear her out, but the truth was that it was Michael she thought of when she spoke.

"I'm sorry. I know it's none of my business. But I also know it's something Michael's been thinking about, and I thought maybe it was on your mind, too. Especially after the way you seemed to be having second thoughts last week about the youth center." She was prattling on, but she couldn't help herself. "Maybe it would help you both to talk about it."

Drew sat silently, his face a mask.

Shannon's pulse went faster the longer he sat without saying anything, and finally she started to push her chair back from the table, feeling sick to her stomach. "I'm sorry. Maybe I should go."

"No." Drew closed his eyes and rested his forehead in one hand, his elbow resting heavily on the table. "Stay, please."

"I think maybe I said too much."

"No, it's just…" He sighed. "Look, I appreciate that you were concerned for me. Truthfully, yes, I did have second thoughts. And third and fourth ones. I grew up in that house, and I have a lot of fond memories of it. The thing is, I don't want it to become some sort of mausoleum for my parents. And I don't think they would want that either. Instead, it's going to be a place full of opportunities for kids who really need them. My parents would like that. Do you know what I mean?"

"Yes," she agreed softly.

"So, no, I'm not having any more second thoughts. My mind is made up. And as far as Michael goes…"

She glanced up at him.

"Maybe he's grown a conscience, but I seriously doubt it. And you know what? I'm really not interested in finding out either way. You say he's been thinking about our parents, feeling guilty maybe? Good. He should feel guilty. Ask him about the things he said before he left next time he asks for your sympathy."

The bitterness in his voice caught her off guard, but not so much that she missed his assumption about his brother. She felt a flicker of defensiveness. "He hasn't been asking for sympathy."

Drew leaned back in his chair and folded his arms across his chest. "Right."

There had been many times in the past when she admired his refusal to compromise on an issue or back down from the stance he had taken. It made him the kind of politician whose promises most people felt they could trust. For the first time, though, it occurred to her that he might be overly stubborn. At least when it came to his brother. "Whatever happened, it happened a long time ago. He was a teenager, right? Teenagers do stupid things all the time. Maybe he's done a lot of growing up since then."

"Not my concern. He's none of my business anymore, and I'm none of his."

She leaned forward. "But he's your *brother*—"

The waiter arrived then to cheerfully deliver their meals, and Shannon stopped speaking. She glanced down at the bowl of soup he slid in front of her. It was not minestrone, but for a moment her memory flashed to the day she dumped her soup on Michael's lap. Then she thought back to the night before and the camaraderie with Michael, and she realized she would be enjoying herself a lot more if he were the one sitting across the table from her, not Drew. The realization hit her with no small amount of surprise.

"The fact he's my brother only means we share the same name, as far as I'm concerned," Drew said tightly after the waiter left.

"What about blood being thicker than water?"

"Those are just words. They may look good in needlepoint, but they don't really mean anything."

Shannon stared at Drew. "Maybe they should."

"You think I'm being unfair." It was a statement, not a question.

She turned her eyes to her soup, feeling her cheeks flush. This was *so* not the way she imagined this week going when it first started. How had everything gotten so off track? "I just think it's a shame," she said finally, feeling suddenly depressed. "For both of your sakes."

Drew leaned in across the table, his expression earnest. "Shannon, you're a good-hearted person and you really believe what you're saying about Michael. You want to see something good in him, and that's admirable. But please—would you, for your own sake, think twice before seeing him again?"

Shannon looked up from her meal to meet his gaze. It was so easy to build up an image of someone, good or bad, and forget there was more to them than that. Drew was guilty of doing that with Michael, but she realized with a surprised sort of dismay that she was guilty of doing that with Drew, too. People were more complicated than that. Drew was a good man, but he wasn't the boy she remembered from high school, not really. And she wasn't the same person either.

She picked up her spoon and gave him a rueful little smile. "No," she said softly and began eating.

• • •

Michael sat at the coffee shop counter and rubbed a hand over tired eyes. He'd spent far more time lying awake last night than sleeping. Not because of Drew, and not because of the youth center, but because of Shannon's parting words to him. Coming from most people, they would have been easy enough to dismiss as politeness or even flattery, but he could tell she meant them and somehow that had been enough to keep him awake hours later.

He drained his second cup of coffee, waiting for the caffeine to kick in. Sure, she meant what she said, but one thing he had learned about Shannon Mahoney was that, despite her sarcasm, she was very innocent in some ways. The truth was she hadn't known him very long, and she couldn't know him very well. Her words to him were sincerely meant but naïve. He wanted to believe them but knew better.

The waitress paused between customers to refill his cup. He picked it up and wondered what it would be like if things were different. If *he* was different.

And he wondered what Shannon was doing now.

He was still thinking about her when he left the coffee shop and returned to his motel room, and when he finally forced his thoughts away from her, they settled on another subject that was just as troubling. Namely, how his chances of getting Drew to listen to him had taken a nosedive since his brother had seen him kissing Shannon. He had blown any chance he might have had with Drew, and if Shannon wasn't able to get through to him, then …

Michael felt a pang. Then he would have failed his parents one last time.

He reached into his wallet for his parents' photograph and studied it as he sank back heavily onto the bed. The picture was well worn around the edges, and each time Michael pulled it out to look at it, he did so a little more carefully than the last time. They were a handsome couple, and the stately house behind them in the photograph was well suited to them in every way. There was pride in the way they carried themselves, a pride he had mistaken for haughtiness once. He had ridiculed it then with the disdain of a teenage boy convinced he had the world all figured out.

"Self-righteous little bastard, weren't you?" Michael murmured to himself as he stared at the picture.

He hadn't been back to the house since the day he left so many years ago. Pride kept him from returning at first, and then guilt after the funeral. Now that he was back in town, more than once he considered going by to see the old place, even if only from the road. Somehow it felt like he hadn't earned that right yet.

There was a knock at his door, and he carefully tucked the picture back into his wallet, mindful of the worn edges.

"Just a minute," he called out as he got up from the bed and ran a hand through his disheveled hair before answering the door.

Shannon stood in the hallway. Apparently after last night's excitement she had abandoned the new clothes in favor of the comfortable familiarity of her old ones, because she was back in sensible slacks now. The hair that he had run through his fingers unbeknownst to her last night was pulled back in the confines of a ponytail. He was tempted to tug it free.

"Hi," she said, and she gave him an uncertain smile. "Can I come in?"

"Of course." He stepped aside to let her pass, acutely aware of her proximity as she moved past him. "So did you get raked over the coals?"

"A little. Not too badly," she admitted, sitting down in the chair. "You're a bad seed, of course, and I'm a wide-eyed twit who doesn't know what's good for her, but other than that things went great."

"Ah." Michael sat down at the foot of the bed across from her.

They sat in awkward silence for a long moment, and Michael wondered if she was thinking about last night. *He* certainly was.

"So, Drew and I talked about you at lunch today," Shannon said finally.

"I'll bet that was an interesting conversation."

"Your brother is very angry with you."

"Yeah, I know."

"Michael…"

He thought he knew what was coming. "Yes?"

"What happened between you and your parents?"

"What did Drew tell you?"

"That you said some things before you left home."

"Yes, I did." Michael got up from the bed and stood beside the window, looking out.

"Maybe I shouldn't ask," she said quietly from behind him.

"I think you've got a right to," Michael told her flatly without turning around. "Considering how I asked you to plead my case for me."

She was silent, not pushing him, for which he was grateful. Would she be so patient with him afterward, he wondered, or would she walk away? He was resigned to being on Drew's blacklist, but he would be sorry to see the same thing happen with Shannon.

"My parents," Michael said finally, "started grooming me as a little kid to take on the Kingston family mantle and everything that went with it. You know, I think I knew my entire family tree before I knew my ABCs. Tradition meant everything to them. You know about my father's political career, right?"

"Sure. People said he could have been the next state senator if…" She trailed off.

"If he had lived, you mean?"

She reddened. "Sorry."

"You've got nothing to apologize for, sweetheart. Yeah, my old man could have probably made it pretty far, and my parents expected the same from me. It was so important to them that I become the best of the best. They had my entire future mapped out for me—looking at colleges before I even started high school, planning a shining political career like my father's. It scared the hell out of me."

He returned to sit on the edge of the bed, but he avoided her eyes. "So what's a kid to do in that situation? Either fall in line or rebel. I chose door number two, and, man, did I do it with style. I guess they hoped it was a phase I'd grow out of. I'd veer off the chosen path, and they'd do everything in their power to steer me back onto it. And the more they tried to rein me in, the harder I tried to break free."

He could feel her eyes on him, but she said nothing.

"It started with just words, you know? Typical teenage rebellion. Refusals, defiance…I guess I thought they weren't taking me seriously, though." He ran a hand through his hair, self-conscious. "So I asked myself, what's every politician's weak spot? Reputation, right? Image. So I hit my dad where it hurt most, or at least that's what I thought at the time. It's hard to impress voters when you've got a juvenile delinquent for a son."

"Juvenile delinquent?" Shannon repeated, confused. "I remember you cut a few classes, but—"

"Oh, I did a lot more than that." Michael smiled humorlessly. "You just never heard about it because Dad found a way to smooth things over every time and keep it out of the papers. A joyride in a 'borrowed' car, some vandalism—and each time I saw the hope in my parents' eyes die a little more."

"You weren't the first kid in the world to get in that kind of trouble."

"Doesn't excuse it, though, does it? The thing is, I never really considered things from their point of view back then. All I saw was a couple of snobs who seemed to be all about superficial things like money, success…image. And I told them so the day I left home. I think my father was too sick of shouting matches to say anything back." Michael stared unseeingly at the wall. "And my mother cried. The last time I ever saw her alive, she was crying."

He stopped then because his voice had started to shake. That final image of his mother was burned into his brain, and he saw it most nights when he closed his eyes.

Shannon's voice was soft. "You couldn't have known that was the last time you'd see them."

"No, of course not." He laughed bitterly. "Because when you're a kid, you're too self-absorbed and stupid to think about things like that. Fact is, my parents died believing I despised them and everything that mattered to them."

"Did you?"

"I thought I did. But I turned out to be a hypocrite."

"What do you mean?"

"I resented them for not respecting what was important to me, but in the end, I guess that's what I did to them, isn't it? My parents were not bad people. Maybe they were a little shallow, maybe not. Maybe they had good reasons for valuing tradition and for expecting great things from their kids. It's too late to ask them about it now, though. And if they had big dreams for me… well, I guess there are a lot worse things parents can do, aren't there?"

She nodded, a grim look on her face.

"So if Drew's angry at me, he's got reason to be. I left quite a mess in his lap when I split. Two shell-shocked parents and the full weight of the Kingston expectations on his shoulders. I wish to God I could take back so many of the things I said and did back then, Shannon, and not just with my parents. But I can't. And the damnable shame of it is that some of this started sinking in before they died. I was just too stubborn to pick up the phone and apologize. You always think there will be plenty of time for that, you know? I wasted so much time. Best I can do now is to try and protect what's left of my parents' legacy." His voice shook despite his best efforts, and he forced a half-smile onto his face. "Can you understand that?"

"Yes."

Michael closed his eyes with a sigh and held his head in his hands.

•••

Go to him, a little voice urged inside Shannon's head. Put your arms around him, hold his hand, but just *do* something. Heaven knew she wanted to, but something held her back. It might have been shyness, but she thought it had more to do with the confusion she had been feeling since her lunch with Drew. She was supposed to want to put her arms around *Drew*, not his brother, but somehow things had changed when she wasn't looking.

What if she went to him and did something stupid? The memory of his mouth on hers last night, even if it was only "pretend," was very vivid at the moment. Emotions were running high now, and emotions could make you do crazy things.

But he looked as if he was expecting her to get up and walk out. Did he really think he was so irredeemable? "Michael…"

He said nothing and didn't look up.

Caution be damned. She couldn't just sit here and watch him heap condemnation on himself like this. Shannon stood up and moved slowly over to the bed to sit beside him. She put a tentative hand on his shoulder, and he stiffened beneath her touch. "Everybody has things in their past they wish they could do over again. You're not a monster because you've made mistakes. You're human."

"But my mistakes have hurt other people very badly."

"Maybe so. But does that make them unforgivable?"

He didn't answer her, but she knew he was thinking *yes*.

"What if it was Drew?" she persisted. "If it were him instead of you, would you hate him?"

"No, but—"

"Then you can't hate yourself either. It's not…it's just not fair."

Now he looked at her, and there was a hint of incredulity in his eyes. "It's not *fair*? This is your argument?"

"Yes," she insisted. "It's a double standard."

The corners of his mouth turned ever so slightly upward, and the sudden warmth in his eyes made her catch her breath. "Shannon, you—" He trailed off, and the burgeoning smile faded.

"I what?"

He shook his head. "Forget it. Don't worry about me. I'm here to try to honor my parents' wishes, not earn forgiveness."

"I think maybe you're here to do both."

"How?" Michael asked softly, and there was such pain in his voice, she wanted to put her arms around him. "They're gone. It's too late for forgiveness."

"You need to forgive yourself."

"I can't."

Unable to help herself any longer, Shannon reached over to take his hand in hers. "If your parents were half the people you say they were, they wouldn't want you to spend the rest of your life punishing yourself, Michael. Don't you think?"

Instead of answering, he closed his fingers around hers and held them tightly. Somehow she didn't think there were any words she could say to convince him she was right. He would have to find a way to work that out for himself.

They sat in silence beside each other for a long time. "You know," Shannon said finally, "I'm really mad at you."

"What?" Michael asked, clearly startled by the turn in their conversation. "You're *mad* at me?"

"Yes." She couldn't quite look him in the eyes as she continued. "When you came to town, I didn't want to like you. You've gone and ruined all that."

He started to laugh, and it was a relief for her to hear something besides sadness in his voice. Pulling his hand free from hers, he put his arm around her shoulders instead and drew her close to his side. She went willingly. "I apologize for making you like me," he said against her temple.

"That's all right."

He swept a runaway lock of her hair back behind her ear with his free hand, then cupped her chin in order to tilt her head up and press his lips to her forehead. She closed her eyes against the sudden fire that swept through her and found herself half hoping his mouth would find its way to hers again like it had last night. "Thank you," he whispered, resting his chin on top of her head.

"For what?' she whispered back.

"Just…thank you."

Her heart did a strange sort of flip inside her chest, and she knew she was in trouble.

Chapter Nine

It was getting increasingly harder to watch Shannon leave, especially knowing she was pining after another man. Michael stood alone in his room after she was gone, looking out his window at the bleak view of trashcans and graffiti but not really seeing any of it. His conversation with Shannon left him feeling drained, but there was a certain relief that went with it, and he wondered if this was what it felt like to emerge from a confessional. It wasn't that he had finally forgiven himself, it was more that she knew the worst of everything now—his past with his parents, his cavalier history with women—and yet, miracle of miracles, she liked him anyway.

Another knock on his door startled him out of his thoughts. Shannon again? His spirits rose at the thought, and he moved quickly to answer the door.

"Long time no—" He froze as he met Drew's eyes. His younger brother stood on his doorstep, glowering coldly at him.

"Unless you'd like a scene out here in the hallway, I suggest you let me come in," Drew said tersely, his jaw clenched.

Old animosities died hard, and Michael had to bite back a bitter and sarcastic response. Wordlessly, he stepped aside to let his brother in, although he suspected Drew cared a lot more about not creating a scene than he did. "How did you find me?" he asked, closing the door after Drew stalked past him.

"Started calling hotels in the phone book."

"Now that's dedication. It must have taken a long time to work your way down to the p's."

"Not really." Drew turned around to face him. "I skipped over the nicer places because I knew I'd find you in a hellhole like this one."

"Oh, it's not so bad," said Michael, eyeing the faded wallpaper and decrepit furniture. "You're just not used to slumming it, little brother."

"No, I suppose you'd be the one to know more about that kind of thing, wouldn't you?"

"Touché."

"What are you doing here, Michael?"

"Renting a room."

Anger flickered over Drew's face. "Don't play games. You know exactly what I mean. What are you really doing back in town?"

"Oh, so now you're interested in talking about that?" Michael returned, feeling some of his own anger spark now. "After you have me banned from your building? Interesting change of heart. What brought it about?"

"Well, I couldn't help but notice you trying to seduce my secretary."

"Sarcasm, huh? Stooping to my level, I see. And it's personal assistant, by the way, not secretary."

"What do you want with Shannon?" Drew asked bluntly.

Her lips, her laughter…everything, Michael thought. But he only raised his eyebrows. "Why? What exactly is she to you, Drew?"

"This has nothing to do with me. I know you, Michael. You see a skirt and you can't resist chasing it. Well, Shannon is not one of your floozies you can have a good time with and then just throw away. She's a nice girl, and I don't want to see her get hurt."

"Yes, she is a nice girl."

"Then if you had half a conscience, you'd leave her alone. Tell me, Michael, are you just using her for kicks, or are you trying to get to me somehow?"

The words would have stung more if there hadn't been some truth to them. Not about using Shannon, but about Michael's blasé attitude toward relationships in the past and about the fact the two of them had made a bargain with each other involving Drew. But the implication that there couldn't possibly be anything else between them hit a nerve. "Shannon is not a diversion, and she's not a puppet," Michael said stiffly. "If you won't give me any credit, at least give her some, would you?"

"Oh, *you're* going to defend her to *me*? That's rich. I give Shannon plenty of credit, but I'm not sure she has enough experience with men to recognize when one of them is bad for her. The thing is, she's been bending my ear about you lately, and about Kingston Manor. And then lo and behold, it turns out you've been—I don't know if *dating* is the right word for it—but you've been hanging around her. Anyway, I'm sure you've been giving her some kind of sob story about how rough life has been for you. Then you sent her in to talk to me, didn't you?"

"Gee, Drew, why would I do that when you've been so agreeable about talking to me directly?"

"So you admit it! You did try to manipulate her," Drew said, his voice rising as he took a step closer to Michael.

"I asked her to listen, and she did, which is more than I can say for you."

"I don't owe—"

"Yeah, yeah, I heard you before. You really hate me so much you couldn't have given me five minutes?"

Drew's eyes were stony. "What I hate, Michael, is what you did to our family."

"Well, that makes two of us."

"Yeah, right."

Michael shook his head warningly. "Don't think you have it all figured out, Drew. Don't think you have *me* figured out. I know just how badly I screwed up. That's why I came back to town. What you're planning to do with the house—"

"You have some nerve—"

"I don't think Mom and Dad would want the home to leave the family. It meant too much to them—"

Drew's fist caught him by surprise as it connected with his chin, and the force of it sent Michael staggering back a step.

For a moment he saw stars, and he shook his head to clear it. He put a hand to his throbbing chin and winced. "Not bad, Drew. Nice to know a desk job hasn't made you go soft. Your constituents know you've got a mean right hook?"

"You don't get to say what Mom and Dad would or would not have wanted. You wouldn't know, would you? Because you left and didn't look back. I'm the one who lived with them, and I'd know what they'd want a hell of a lot more than you would."

"Maybe," Michael said, letting his hand fall away from his chin. "But just for the record, was that punch for them or for Shannon?"

"It was for me," Drew returned darkly, his hand still curled in a fist.

"Feel better now, or did you want to take another shot?" Michael took a step closer until he was only inches away from his younger brother.

"Just stay away from Shannon. In fact, why don't you pack your bags and leave town altogether? There's no place for you here anymore. God knows I don't want to see you again."

Michael said nothing. The words were hardly a surprise, but there was a finality to them that hit him hard. For just a moment he thought he caught a glimpse of the little boy his brother used to be in the angry man before him, and he felt a sudden ache in his chest. There was a time, when they were both kids, that Drew had looked up to him and he had looked after Drew, protecting him from school bullies and initiating him in all the rites of passage that went along with boyhood. Then the glimpse was gone, and all he saw was the bitterness in his brother's eyes.

Drew might have taken his silence for acquiescence. In any case, he pushed past Michael and walked out without another word, slamming the door firmly shut behind him. Michael stood frozen, dimly aware that his chin still throbbed. Finally, moving as if in a daze, he grabbed a towel from the bathroom and went out to get some ice from the ice machine. He wrapped it up in the towel and applied it to his chin, wincing.

The chances of persuading Drew to change his mind about the youth center were slim to none now, he acknowledged as he laid back on his bed and stared up at the ceiling. The room grew darker as twilight fell, but he didn't bother turning on a light. Shannon's chances with Drew seemed to be a lot better than his given Drew's protectiveness toward her tonight, a realization that left a sour taste in Michael's mouth. It was what Shannon wanted, and he should have been happy for her.

He was not.

It could have been bitterness that made him feel that way, or resentment. After all, she was within reach of her desires and he was not, but he was honest enough with himself to admit that wasn't it. The thought of Drew touching her in anything more than a casual way made his gut tighten.

Because, selfish SOB that he was, Michael wanted her for himself. As penance, he pressed the ice harder against his chin until the pressure hurt, leaving it there as the evening air darkened around him.

Chapter Ten

The wise thing to do was to stay away from Shannon for a while. Not because of Drew's warning, but because Michael needed to get his head on straight. Maybe it was just a matter of proximity, and if he put a little distance between them it would be much easier to put things into perspective, including the feelings she inspired in him.

Of course he liked her. What was there not to like? She was funny, warm, and made him laugh more lately than he had in a long time. And there was something very sweet and innocent about her, something that brought out an urge in him to protect her from disappointment.

And catty girls, he thought with a wry smile, remembering the evening at the park.

But thinking about that evening might have been a mistake, because it made him recall other things that happened that night, too. Like kissing her and holding her hand beneath the stars while they talked about high school memories. For a kiss that was only for show, it lingered in his head far more than it should have.

But she was an appealing woman, after all, and he was a red-blooded, heterosexual male. It was perfectly natural for him to feel some kind of attraction to her. It hardly meant his feelings went any deeper than that.

Except lately she filled his head more and more, and it was harder for him to explain that realization away. It was possible it was the reprieve she offered from his self-loathing that he welcomed, and the comfort that her presence gave him. It was possible he just liked himself better when he was with her. But it was also possible he simply wanted a woman who didn't want him back.

He could make her want him, a little voice in the back of his mind suggested slyly. Seduction was his specialty, wasn't it? With a little effort, he might lure her attention away from Drew and find out what happened when he kissed her for real.

Michael stared at himself in the mirror. "Bastard," he said softly to his reflection. "Would you really do that to her?" Because, in the end, he was not the kind of man who could make her happy, and certainly not the kind of man she deserved. Drew was a much better match for her, and to all appearances, his brother finally seemed to be noticing that fact. "Let her go," he told himself harshly, and he turned away from the mirror.

Yes, the smart thing for him to do would be to keep his distance from her. And for two whole days, he did just that—although he found himself checking his cell phone frequently for any missed calls from her. But the longer his internal debate raged on, the more his resolve to stay away from her weakened, especially when the only other thing to think about was his failure to save his parents' house.

Maybe, alone in his motel room with nothing but his own thoughts, he was building his feelings for Shannon up into much more than they really were. Maybe once he was around her again, he would see that his affection for her was just that: affection. And maybe spending a little time with her would help him to understand just how unrealistic a pair they would make.

Besides, he owed her a thank-you for her efforts to get Drew to listen, even if Drew did refuse to budge in his way of thinking. It was a transparent excuse to see her, but he forced that thought from his mind.

Tomorrow. He would just drive by for a minute, that was all. Just long enough to prove to himself there was nothing going on between himself and Shannon outside of his imagination. Plain and simple.

Sure.

· · ·

The clock on the wall finally read five o'clock.

Thank you, God.

By the time Friday afternoon had rolled around, Shannon's stomach was one big knot. Two days of avoiding eye contact with both Clarissa and Drew had taken a toll, and the few words she exchanged with either of them were brief and all business. Once or twice Drew seemed as if he might want to say something else, something more personal, but in the end he kept it to himself, for which Shannon was immensely grateful.

Clarissa had said little, too, but even now Shannon could feel the weight of the look the older woman had been giving her all day. Steeling herself, Shannon looped her purse strap over her shoulder and walked past her friend's desk on the way to the exit.

"Shannon."

Taking a deep breath, Shannon halted and turned back to look at Clarissa.

They stared at each other in silence for a moment before Clarissa finally sighed and shook her head. "You're still seeing him, aren't you?"

Only every time I close my eyes, Shannon thought, her stomach churning again and not entirely because of her friend's scrutiny. She said nothing, but her gaze dropped away from Clarissa's.

"What kind of happy ending do you see happening here, honey? He's a player. There's no future in it."

"There is no 'it', Clarissa," Shannon said tersely, finding her voice. "There never was. You have nothing to worry about. Trust me."

The older woman raised her eyebrows.

"I mean it, really." Shannon adjusted her purse strap again, more out of nerves than necessity. "I'll see you Monday." She turned to go, moving quickly before Clarissa could offer any further cautionary advice.

As she got in her car, though, her friend's words warred with her already jumbled feelings regarding what had happened with Michael. For a moment her hand hovered over her cell phone. She was torn between the desire to see if he was all right after the other night's confession and her fear that if she spoke to him he would be able to tell that it was more than just friendly concern on her part. And then what? He was Michael Kingston, after all, and she was just plain-Jane Shannon Mahoney. She was not the kind of woman to hold a man's interest, not in that way. Clarissa was right. What did she really expect to happen?

She moved her hand away from the phone and put her key in the ignition.

• • •

It was a beautiful Saturday afternoon. The air was pleasantly warm without being too hot, and Michael drove with the windows of his truck rolled down. His grip on the steering wheel was tighter than usual, and he forced himself to relax it. As he pulled into Shannon's driveway, he listened for sounds of power tools but heard only the sounds of nature. Her truck was parked in the drive, but maybe she wasn't at home. Maybe she was even out with Drew.

He got out of the truck and headed for her front steps, half-expecting her dog to come around the corner of the house again with tail wagging, but the animal didn't appear. There was no answer to Michael's knock on the door, and, disappointed, he was about to turn around and go the way he had come when he heard a dog barking, followed by Shannon's laughter. It was a rare sound, and he let it wash over him now, uncomfortably aware that his reaction to it was not a platonic one.

He was playing with fire by coming here.

Michael followed the sound of her laughter off the porch and around to the back of the house, stopping before Shannon saw him. The half-finished deck was now completely finished, and while Bo leaped off the edge of it to fetch a stick, Shannon sat on the railing where it met the side of the house. She looked as if she had just stepped out of a shower with her hair still damp and hanging freely past her shoulders, and for a moment he thought she was dressed only in an oversized T-shirt before he caught a glimpse of short denim cutoffs barely visible beneath the hem. One knee was bent close to her chest while the other leg, shapely and lean, dangled temptingly over the edge of the railing. Michael's eyes traced the contours of it, and his pulse quickened.

Resting her chin on her bent knee, Shannon laughed again as Bo pounced on the stick and shook it vigorously. "Pretty fierce, Bo," she called out, unaware of Michael's presence as the wide neck of her T-shirt slid to expose one shoulder. She combed the fingers of one hand idly through her wet hair, working out a tangle. "Poor stick didn't stand a chance."

His gaze went immediately to her bare shoulder. Just friends, Michael thought grimly. Sure. Who was he kidding?

She was so natural and unselfconscious that he was reluctant to disturb her, particularly since he had a heavy feeling there wouldn't be many more moments like this between them before he left town. The heaviness grew stronger as he studied her. There was a world of difference between her and every other woman he had known in his life, and the way he wanted her was very different, too. True, he wanted to touch her, taste her, feel her against him, but there was something more to it, something unfamiliar to him. It was unsettling, so he quickly reminded himself that none of it mattered anyway. She wanted Drew, and she seemed to be getting her wish. As her partner in all of this, he ought to be congratulating her. And then he ought to forget about everything else.

He cleared his throat, and she looked up. Her look of surprise melted into one of obvious pleasure, and he felt his determination to stay detached wavering.

She smiled a little self-consciously. "Hey."

"Hey." Michael approached the deck, running one hand on the railing. "Nice work."

"Thanks," she said, looking pleased.

Bo dropped his stick and trotted over to sniff Michael's hand, tail wagging. Michael rubbed the dog's ears until a sound in the underbrush caught Bo's attention, and the dog jogged off to investigate.

"Want to come up?" Shannon invited him, with a hint of shy pride in her voice. "Check out the view?"

He already was, although it was not the view she meant. With one hand on the railing, he climbed slowly up the steps, cautioning himself not to get too close to her for fear of doing something foolish. "Very nice," he said, reaching the top and turning to look out at the unspoiled nature surrounding her house. "You've got your own little slice of paradise here."

"Yeah, I like it." She came over to stand next to him, stopping before she got very close, for which he was grateful. "It's one thing to try and picture the finished product in your head, but seeing the reality is another thing altogether. There's just something about it that's so…"

"Satisfying?"

She nodded. "That's a good word for it." Turning her head, she looked up at him hesitantly. "Are you okay? I mean, after everything you said the other night, I was wondering if things were a little…raw, maybe."

With an effort, he was able to keep his tone breezy. "I'm fine. Actually, I wanted to stop in and offer my congratulations to you."

Her brow furrowed. "For what?"

"Drew."

"Oh." A strange look crossed her face, and she looked away for a moment. "I think that might be a little premature."

"I don't think so. He came to see me at the motel."

"He did?"

"Been a long time since I've seen him that hot under the collar. Normally he's more ice than fire with me, but not then." He rubbed his bruised chin at the memory of his brother's fist. "Hence congratulations. He's clearly worked up about you." He forced a smile on his face.

Shannon made a noncommittal sort of sound.

"What, you don't believe me? You still don't think you could catch a guy's eye like that? Trust me, sweetheart, you can."

But she said nothing, and that strange look flickered over her face again.

"And he would be very lucky to have you." Michael cleared his throat again, remembering the way it felt to put his arm around her and the way she fit against his side. He shouldn't be thinking about things like that right now. "So, listen, I wanted to say thank you for trying to get Drew to listen about the youth center. I know I put you in a difficult spot, and I'm sorry about that."

"It's okay. Did he finally talk to you about it, then?"

The vivid blue-green of her eyes was very distracting, especially when those eyes were focused so fully on him. Michael took a few steps away from her, pretending he was examining her handiwork on the deck but really needing to put more distance between them before he did something rash. Like pull her to him. "I'm not sure you could really call it talking, but, yes, the subject came up. I wouldn't exactly say it went all that great."

"Oh." She hesitated a moment. "What happened?"

"Well, he made it pretty clear the youth center is a done deal." He stared unseeingly at the trees dotting the landscape around her house. "Among other things."

"I'm sorry."

He shrugged with a lack of concern that wasn't what he really felt.

"Michael?"

He turned around to look at her, and the sympathy on her face made it hard for him to maintain his casual air.

"You must be feeling pretty disappointed about it, but maybe— maybe it's not as bad as you think."

She took a step toward him, and the breeze carried the scent of her hair and skin to him, fresh and clean from her shower. He groaned inwardly, trying not to let her see the effect it had on him. If she came much closer …

"It's just that I've been thinking about something Drew said at lunch the other day, about what he thinks the youth center could be. You've been trying to protect that house in order to honor your parents' legacy, but maybe the youth center can actually be a way to do that. I mean, you and Drew want the same thing really, even if you're going about it in different ways."

"Do we?" he asked softly. She didn't seem to notice the way his eyes flickered over her as he spoke.

"You want the things that mattered to your parents to be preserved, right? Hard work, integrity, excellence…Those are things kids can learn about at the Kingston Youth Center, and it's all because of your parents. Lots of children who might not have had the opportunity otherwise will have their lives enriched because of your mom and dad. The house itself, that's just wood and bricks. Eventually it will crumble to dust, but the effect it will have had on the lives of so many kids—well, who can really imagine how far an impact like that can go?"

He knew her words were intended to be comforting, which he appreciated, but it was also clear to him she meant every word of what she said. She wasn't making speeches just to make him feel better. "Maybe," he said finally. "Maybe they would have liked that. I don't know if it's enough, but it looks as though it will have to be."

"You didn't fail, Michael. You didn't let them down."

He laughed bitterly under his breath. "That's debatable."

"You didn't!" When he only shrugged, Shannon's expression turned stern. "Would you stop trying to turn yourself into a villain? It doesn't suit you."

"Are you reprimanding me?"

"Somebody has to."

In spite of the fact their conversation centered on the less-than-joyful topic of his failings as a son, Michael felt his mouth turn up at the corners. Her schoolmarm tone of rebuke was somewhat offset by her just-stepped-out-of-the-shower appearance, especially her wind-tousled hair. "So you're going to scold me into feeling better about myself?"

She looked a little embarrassed. "Well, maybe."

God, he was going to miss her. "Only you could do that, you know, sweetheart." His grin grew.

Blushing faintly and shrugging, she returned his smile.

Their eyes met again, not a problem in and of itself. The problem was that they held each other's gazes a little too long. One of them should have looked away by now, and if she wouldn't do it, then he ought to. But when had he ever been able to do the right thing?

For her sake, it was time for him to start.

Michael tore his eyes away from Shannon's and turned back to look at the landscape before they could focus on something dangerous, like her mouth. "It's time for me to leave," he said finally.

"Leave? But you just got here."

"I mean leave town."

"What?"

He heard dismay in her voice, and he hated himself for the spark of hope it gave him. Such feelings were best squelched immediately. "I did promise to walk away if Drew refused to change his mind, remember?" he returned lightly. "I'd like to think I'm a man of my word."

"Well, yeah…but—"

"I came to town to try to change my brother's mind. That didn't happen. I may have to live with that, but there's no reason for me to stick around now and watch the fallout, is there?"

"Oh. I suppose not."

The silence hung heavily in the air.

He could kiss her, that seductive little voice in his head whispered to him. Right now. Just turn around and pull her to him. And then she might forget about Drew. Because she was innocent and inexperienced when it came to passion, not like Michael. And passion might make her forget what she really wanted.

His body started to turn back around toward her almost of its own accord, and Michael dug his fingers into the wooden railing to stop himself. For once in his life, damn it, he was going to do the right thing. Shannon deserved her happy ever after, and Drew was the one who could give it to her. Drew was the good one, not Michael. If Shannon was feeling any kind of confusion about her feelings, it was time to take himself out of the equation and clear things up for her.

Even if the idea of her putting her arms around his brother made his gut churn.

Michael forced what was probably a poor excuse for a smile onto his face and turned back around.

Shannon's eyes were downcast. She opened her mouth as if to speak, but seemed to struggle with whether or not to do so.

It might be best for both of them if she didn't, Michael thought. His control over himself was weak enough as it was. "So…thanks. For everything. You more than held up your end of the bargain."

She finally nodded without looking up.

He pried his fingers from the railing and took a step away from her.

"Michael?"

His traitorous body froze immediately. "Yes?"

"Maybe...you could stay a little longer."

"Why?"

She hesitated. "Well, for your brother."

He felt a flicker of disappointment. "Drew? I can't get out of town fast enough for him."

"I mean...maybe it's possible for you two to patch things up. He is your brother, after all. I think deep down he means a lot to you."

"He does."

"So isn't it worth trying to fix things between you two?"

Michael's smile was more genuine this time, but far from happy. "I don't think that's in the cards, sweetheart. It's best if I leave now."

She looked as if she wanted to say more. Before she could, he risked the effects of her proximity on his senses and leaned in to kiss her on the cheek. It was a foolish chance to take, and he felt the sharp pull of desire as his lips touched the softness of her skin, but he allowed himself this last temptation because he knew he wouldn't see her again after today. Selfish to the end, he thought. For a moment neither of them moved, and he breathed in the scent of her, his cheek brushing hers. A slight turn of her head, and his mouth would find hers in a second. Then he would be lost.

He forced himself to step back from her. Her eyes on him were so wide. It had been a mistake to come here, but if he left now maybe he could avoid causing irreparable damage. "Take care of yourself, Shannon. Make sure Drew appreciates what he's got, all right?"

He gave her one more forced smile before finally descending the steps from the deck.

•••

Shannon's eyes followed Michael as he walked away from the deck. Away from her. It wasn't like she hadn't expected this, on some level at least. She wasn't a fool or anything. He had been quite up front from the beginning: he was in town for one reason only—to protect his family's home—and now that reason had disintegrated. Sure, they might have spent a little time together, but had she really expected that to change anything? Of course not, she thought with a lump in her throat. Not really.

But maybe she had hoped a little. The other night in his room had been so innocent on the surface, but it had been enough to leave her emotions a jumbled up mess. It's not like he *had* to feel the same way that she did or anything, but —

Surely he must feel something? Surely there was something different in his manner with her today. His smile had no joy behind it when he said goodbye to her.

Only because of his failure with his brother, her inner voice taunted her. Not because of her.

But then the way he kissed her cheek…Shannon's fingers touched her face where his lips had been a moment ago. Funny how the simplest of touches between them could have such a profound effect on her. Was it really so crazy to think it might have some kind of impact on him, too?

She took a step forward as if to go after him, wishing she knew the answer and wishing she had the guts to call after him.

Stay.

Stay because I want you to. Stay because you want me, too.

But her feet went no further, and Shannon's mouth refused to form any of the words that were raging through her mind.

When she tried, they were drowned out by the old familiar voice of self-doubt.

He couldn't possibly feel the same way you do. Are you kidding? He's Michael Kingston, every woman's fantasy come to life.

What are you?

So she watched him walk away, her mouth still struggling to speak.

And failing.

Woman of confidence. Right, she thought miserably.

• • •

Michael shoved the last of his belongings in his duffel bag with more force than was necessary. There was one more person he needed to see before he left town. Slinging his hastily packed bag over his shoulder, he headed for the motel parking lot and his truck. One way or another, he was going to find a way to talk to Drew, even if he had to wait outside his apartment building all night.

There was a different doorman outside than the one who had barred his entrance here before, but he looked every bit as rigid as the last one. The residents here no doubt paid a small fortune to guarantee their privacy, and they certainly got their money's worth. Michael's most realistic option might very well be to spend the night in his truck in hopes of catching his brother on the way out the next day. Hopefully he wouldn't have to resort to that.

"Good evening, sir," the uniformed man greeted him politely with a bearing that would have made any military man proud. "Are you here to see one of our tenants?"

Michael stopped before him and glanced up at the rows of windows above them both. "Drew Kingston."

"Is Mr. Kingston expecting you, sir?"

"No," Michael said with a humorless laugh. "I seriously doubt it. But it's very important that I speak to him."

The man's smile grew a little cooler. "And you are?"

"His brother. There's a good chance he'll tell you to kick my butt to the curb, but please, tell him I said he was right and I'm taking his advice, but I need to see him before I leave. Tell him it's about Shannon."

"One moment."

Michael turned away and stared into the darkening evening air, his hands stuffed into the front pockets of his jeans. After tonight, would he be likely to come back and see this city or Drew again? Or Shannon? his inner voice echoed. No, he thought with a pang. Not for a very long time, if ever. People here were better off the farther he stayed away from them. But he wished he could have had a little more time before having to say good-bye to Shannon.

"Sir?"

The sound of the doorman's voice made Michael turn back around.

"Mr. Kingston says you may go up."

He felt a flicker of relief. "Thank you."

It was a classy place, the décor tasteful and elegant without going over the top. Probably not the kind of place a city councilman could afford if he didn't come from old money, Michael thought as he rode up in the elevator. But he didn't begrudge his brother his inheritance. Drew would no doubt manage it much better than he would have, and Michael wouldn't feel comfortable living in luxury like this. No, his apartment over his bar suited him much better, although the thought of going back to it now didn't appeal to him as much as it would have a week or two ago.

Stepping out of the elevator, Michael searched for the right apartment number. There was a long wait after his knock, almost as if Drew had changed his mind about seeing him, but the door finally opened, and his brother greeted him with a stony stare.

"Thanks for letting me in," Michael said evenly. "I wasn't sure you would."

"Neither was I."

"Can I come in?"

The younger Kingston hesitated, not looking overly thrilled.

"I won't stay long."

Wordlessly, Drew turned and let Michael follow him inside. "So was there any truth to what you told my doorman, or was it a line of bull to get in and hassle me about the house some more?" Drew asked coolly, pouring himself a drink but pointedly not offering one to Michael.

"No bull. I'm leaving town. And as far as the house goes…" Michael gave a half-hearted shrug. "I may not agree with what you're choosing to do with it, but I understand your reasons a little better now. I'm sure you'll turn that place into something good. Something that will *do* a lot of good."

"And what prompted this little change of heart?" Drew asked warily, clearly not convinced that Michael was sincere.

"Shannon."

They stood in silence for a while, sizing each other up. Knowing he might not get this chance again, Michael struggled to make his next words count.

"Drew…I want to say that I'm sorry. For hurting Mom and Dad the way I did, for leaving you to pick up the pieces when I left—I shouldn't have done that. I thought I had my reasons for leaving, but I handled things badly. Very badly. I'm sorry."

His brother continued to watch him with a skeptical look on his face.

Fair enough, Michael thought. He supposed he deserved it. "I think about Mom and Dad a lot, Drew. Hard to believe, I'm sure, but I do. You look a lot like Dad, you know that?" Michael smiled wanly. "Right down to your suit and tie. They would be proud of you. Proud of who you turned out to be." His smiled faded. "You were right. You would know what they wanted a lot better than I would. So, no, I won't give you any more grief about the youth center."

"Good," Drew said stiffly.

"And about Shannon—" Michael's gaze dropped. "She's a very special person."

"Yes, she is."

"And she likes you. A lot. Be good to her, okay? And make sure she's happy."

Drew's brow furrowed.

"That's all I came to say. I'll get out of your hair now." Michael turned to go, but then he paused and looked back at his little brother, who wore a bemused expression on his face that sparked childhood memories. Michael smiled faintly, and a little sadly, too. "Do you remember that old apple tree we used to climb when we were kids?"

"Yes," said Drew, clearly startled by the change in topic. "Why?"

"Do you remember the day you finally reached the top?"

"I got stuck." Drew's voice was quiet. "You had to help me down."

"Sure I did, because I was the one who convinced you to climb it in the first place, and I knew Mom and Dad would kill me if they found out." Michael stared at his brother, once again catching a glimpse of the boy he used to be. "But we both made it down okay. And you were pretty damned proud of yourself, too."

"Yes, I was."

"Do me a favor, Drew. Remember the good stuff, too." Michael opened the door to go. "And when it's the right time, please tell Shannon…"

"Tell her what?"

It was a sentence he couldn't bring himself to finish. "Never mind. Take care of yourself, Drew. And her, too."

And Michael closed the door behind him, leaving Drew to frown speculatively after him.

Chapter Eleven

Shannon stared at the ceiling in her bedroom as darkness finally gave way to the grayness of dawn. She didn't want to think about Michael, so naturally what had she done all night? Think about Michael. There had been an ache in her heart ever since he had left town a couple of weeks ago that seemed to get worse every time she replayed her last conversation with him in her head.

Should she have said something? But what if he didn't feel the same way about her?

What if he did? Was it really so crazy that he might?

Most likely, yes.

She should have said something.

Shannon groaned and rolled over, throwing her pillow over her face. Beside her, Bo made a disgruntled sound before resettling himself on her bedspread. "Sorry, Bo," Shannon muttered, her voice muffled by her pillow. "Don't let my existential crisis disturb you."

He didn't, because a moment later he was snoring.

Shannon wrapped her arms tightly around her pillow, her face still buried in it. How had this happened? She had been perfectly happy before Michael showed up. Well, maybe not perfectly, but she hadn't had this aching in her heart. Wistfulness, sure. Maybe a little longing and loneliness as far as Drew was concerned, but nothing like this dull kind of hurt that just didn't seem to go away. What had happened to her?

She'd fallen hard, that's what happened to her.

Shannon took a deep breath and felt it hitch in her throat. Unattainable men. She certainly knew how to pick them, didn't she?

The sigh she let out made Bo snort awake again. The dog made an irritable grumbling kind of sound and leaped down from the bed in exasperation to go search for a quieter place to sleep.

Shannon tossed the pillow aside and stared at the ceiling again. Coward, she thought hollowly to herself. You should have said something. You shouldn't have just let him walk away like that. Story of your life.

Because there was something there. Surely it hadn't all been in her imagination. There was real warmth in his smile when he turned it on her.

But this was Michael Kingston she was talking about here. He knew how to get a woman if he wanted her, knew what kind of moves to make. If he had wanted her, he could have had her. In a heartbeat.

If.

Her alarm clocked beeped at her, and she reached over without looking to switch it off before lying still again.

If he had wanted her.

The ache in her chest grew more pronounced. Throwing off the bedspread, Shannon pushed herself up and out of bed just to try and divert her attention elsewhere. She knew by now that a hot shower—or maybe a cold one—and some breakfast would do little to distract her thoughts from what ailed her, but she would go through the motions nevertheless. And hope that maybe sometime soon the hurt would start to lessen.

• • •

"Drew Kingston's office, Shannon speaking. How may I help you?" Her voice was flat and listless even to her own ears, but

Shannon was unable to fake any amount of enthusiasm. "Please hold a moment."

"Shannon?"

Shannon glanced up to see Clarissa hovering in the doorway. The older woman wore an expression of concern on her face.

"Honey, is everything all right?"

"Everything's fine."

"It would be easier to believe that if I'd seen you smile even once in the past two weeks." Clarissa frowned, peering closer. "And those shadows under your eyes keep getting darker. Not sleeping much, are you?"

Shannon shrugged noncommittally and pressed the intercom button for Drew's office. "Phone call for you on line one. Zoning issue." She released the button without waiting for a response from Drew and turned her attention back to her computer. Outwardly, at least.

"Oh, Shannon, won't you please talk to *somebody*?"

"Nothing to talk about."

"Liar," Clarissa returned gently.

Shannon made no further comment, and Clarissa finally gave up and returned to her own desk, frowning worriedly and shaking her head. Pulling up a random file on her screen to appear busy, Shannon took a slow, deep breath.

She was no stranger to unrequited feelings, but this time it seemed to cut more deeply. Maybe because a part of her had been naïve enough to actually hope something had affected Michael at least a little like it affected her. And so it wasn't just that she felt unwanted or undesirable, but she felt foolish, too. Very, very foolish.

Her eyes grew wet, and she swiveled in her chair to reach for a tissue. As she did so, she met Drew's gaze, standing in the now open doorway of his office. She blinked quickly to try to hide the moisture in her eyes. "I thought you had a phone call."

"I asked him to call back. Shannon, would you come into my office for a minute? I'd like to talk to you."

She scrambled to think of an excuse that would let her avoid conversation, suspecting the topic would have something to do with Michael. "But the phone—"

Drew looked past her to where Clarissa's desk was. "Clarissa? Could you keep an eye on the phone for a few minutes?"

The older woman glanced first at him and then at Shannon. "Absolutely. Take all the time you need."

Drew looked back at Shannon. "Come on," he said gently. "Please?"

Avoiding his eyes, Shannon got up and walked slowly past him into his office.

"Have a seat," he invited her, closing the door behind him. She sank into the chair across from his desk, still avoiding his gaze as he sat on the desk's edge near her. He fidgeted with his tie for a few moments, something he usually did when he was struggling to think of the right words to say. "Shannon, I'll be honest. I'm worried about you."

"I'm fine."

"I don't think you are fine. I think you've been hurting ever since Michael left. As his brother, I—"

"You feel a certain responsibility?" she finished for him.

He played with his tie again. "Yes. Yes, I do. And as your boss. And maybe as a friend, too. It just seems that despite what you said the last time we talked about him, you two were doing more than just spending a little time together. And I think maybe you fell pretty hard for Michael."

She felt her eyes tearing up and started blinking again. Wordlessly, Drew reached for a tissue and handed it to her. "Thanks," she said with difficulty, inwardly wincing at the slight catch in her voice.

"It might help you to talk about it."

Shannon started to open her mouth and then closed it again.

Drew nudged her with his elbow. "Try it. I'm a world-class listener when I put my mind to it."

She gave him another wan smile. Her heart no longer leaped when Drew was around, but he was still an all-around good guy. "I think maybe I owe you an apology," she said finally, drying her eyes on the tissue.

"Me? No."

"I wasn't completely honest with you about why I was..." She faltered. "...hanging around your brother. We had a kind of arrangement."

"Because he wanted you to help him with the youth center." Drew nodded. "I figured that much out for myself."

"I thought it was for the best," she said quickly, hoping he would understand what she meant. "He made some good points but there was too much bad blood between the two of you for you to consider them."

He smiled reassuringly. "It's okay, Shannon. Truthfully, I had some of the same concerns as Michael at one point. You don't need to apologize for anything."

"That's not quite all there was to it." Shannon folded and refolded the tissue in her hand. Maybe she ought to be mortified at the thought of admitting the crush she had on Drew, but now that it was gone, it didn't seem to matter so much anymore. Or maybe she was just too depressed to care. She smiled faintly and made herself look him in the eye. "You know, I had quite the crush on you in high school. Along with fifty million other girls."

He looked a little surprised. "You did?"

"Yes. All four years. And the truth is—" Now her face did grow a little warmer. "For a long time after you came to work here, I thought I still did. But I think now it was more because I was still sort of mixed up about high school than anything else. No offense," she added hastily.

"None taken," he said, and she could tell he was trying not to smile.

"The thing is, Michael spotted it right away." She grew somber again. "And in exchange for my help, he offered to sort of... mentor me."

"I see."

"I'm sorry. I guess it was a little shady."

Now he did smile. "Shady? I've seen a lot worse, Shannon. I am in politics, after all."

"You're trying to make me feel better, aren't you?"

"I am." He studied her more seriously. "So, somewhere along the way things changed, huh?"

Shannon was quiet for a minute. She wiped her eyes again. "I feel like an idiot," she said finally.

"Why?"

"Because..." She shrugged helplessly, unable to get the words out.

"Because you started to have feelings for Michael?" he suggested gently.

She bit her lip and nodded. "I should have known better."

"We can't help who we care about."

"But I should have known better than to think..."

"Think what?"

She felt her breath hitch in her throat. "Never mind. I guess I just started to imagine something that wasn't there. So, therefore," she pointed at herself, "idiot."

"Shannon..." Drew appeared to weigh his next words carefully. "I'm not sure if I should say this or not."

"Say what?"

"Michael came to see me the night he left town. Only briefly, but he was different."

Shannon looked at him, confused at where he was going with this.

"He said some things about our parents. And about you. God knows I'm not my brother's biggest fan, but I think he actually meant what he said." Drew ran a hand through his hair, frowning slightly. "What I'm trying to say is I suspect you may have had a bigger effect on him than you realize."

She looked away again. "I seriously doubt that."

Drew was silent for a long time. "You might be selling yourself a little short," he said finally.

He was making an admirable effort to cheer her up, so for his sake, she tried to smile. "Maybe." She stood up. "I should get back to work. Thanks for the tissue."

"Why don't you just call it a day? It's nearly that time anyway."

"Thanks. Maybe I will."

"Hey, Shannon?"

At the door, she turned around.

"It's a shame I didn't know about your crush in high school." He grinned boyishly at her. "That could have been interesting."

She smiled back. "Yeah, it could have."

And then she closed the door behind her.

• • •

Michael's head throbbed from the noise in the bar. Noise was good. It meant there were lots of customers, which was always welcome news for a business owner like himself, but tonight it was more jarring than reassuring, and he felt a need to escape from it. Since getting back from his trip he had tried to throw himself into work as much as possible, thinking it would be the best medicine for him until his feelings for Shannon went away. Only problem was, those feelings weren't cooperating.

Behind the bar, he absently mixed a couple of drinks before realizing the voluptuous brunette on the other side of it had asked him a question. She was now frowning at him impatiently as she waited for a reply he was apparently late in giving.

"Sorry," he acknowledged with a curt smile. "What was that?"

She leaned forward a bit, displaying a generous amount of cleavage for his benefit. "I said I'll bet you probably know some great places around here where two people who wanted to be alone together could have some fun." Her eyelashes fluttered coyly as her lips parted in a smile that was clearly an invitation. "What time are you off?"

He turned away from the flesh she had out on display and focused again on the drinks. "Late. I'm closing up tonight."

"I can wait—"

"Afraid not," he returned firmly, smiling a little to take some of the sting out of the rejection. "Thanks anyway."

Her eyes narrowed, and she stalked off toward the other end of the bar, muttering something he was pretty sure wasn't very polite.

Michael caught the eye of the other bartender on duty, Sammy. "Are you nuts?" Sammy mouthed at him, jerking his head in the direction of the departing brunette and raising his eyebrows. Michael just shrugged halfheartedly before gesturing that he was heading to the back room. Sammy nodded and leaned forward to take a drink order from a couple at the bar.

The tiny back room was cramped and cluttered, but at least it offered some relief from the noise of the crowd. Michael closed the door behind him and sank wearily into a chair behind the desk covered with assorted papers and invoices. And the hometown newspaper Drew would probably be shocked to know he subscribed to.

He rubbed his aching head and glanced at the article he had clipped out earlier that day.

Kingston Youth Center Dedication Ceremony To Be Held Tomorrow.

The headline seemed to cut through him every time he read it. Partly because it reminded him of his failure to change his brother's mind, although he did his best to adopt Drew's perspective on the matter, but mostly because it made him think of who would almost certainly be attending the ceremony.

He averted his eyes from the article and stared into space. Would Shannon be there merely in a professional capacity, or would she be going as Drew's date? He pictured her on his brother's arm, smiling into Drew's eyes, and his gut tightened.

Was this what it was like to really want a woman? Was this what love songs were all written about? If so, it was awful. Love wasn't bliss, it was misery. To want something so much and know it wasn't yours to hold, to touch ...

For a moment his old instincts flared up again. He could have seduced her away from Drew if he really tried. Maybe he still could.

No. He couldn't. Maybe he could have not so long ago, but not now. Not to her.

Michael abruptly crumpled the article and forced his attention to the waiting stack of invoices.

• • •

It was a good-sized crowd that was gathering on the grounds of the Kingston family estate. Townspeople, families, reporters—even a news camera, Shannon realized as she spotted it near the far side of the podium, its lens focused on the ceremonial ribbon stretched out before the entrance to the house. Drew had to be pleased by the amount of community interest in today's ceremony. It boded well for the future of the youth center.

As if on cue, Drew appeared then to take his place at the podium. He glanced at a large framed picture of his parents that had been placed on an easel nearby, and a flicker of emotion crossed his face that might have been sadness or maybe just nostalgia. Whatever it was, he quickly replaced it with a smile as he turned his full attention to the crowd before him.

"Ladies and gentlemen," he began, "I want to thank you all for coming out today to help me celebrate what I hope will be the beginning of a wonderful new chapter in the support of our community's children: the Kingston Youth Center."

There was a smattering of applause.

Shannon joined in politely but was well aware that she was doing little more than going through the motions. Enough, she berated herself. This day had been a long time in coming, and Drew had worked hard to make it happen. It was a good and selfless thing that he was doing, and she ought to be thinking about that instead of remembering Michael's disappointment in himself over what he saw as his failure to atone for the past.

But her heart still ached for him. She searched the crowd for Michael, on the off chance he had decided to attend after all, but he was not there. She hadn't really expected him to be.

Drew's voice caught Shannon's attention again, and she forced her thoughts away from Michael. "My parents, Blythe and Walter Kingston," he glanced at the portrait again, "worked hard to ensure I had opportunities. Opportunities in education, opportunities in sports, opportunities to achieve." He looked back at the faces in the crowd. "Many children never get such opportunities. For them, dreams are a luxury they cannot afford."

Shannon watched him turn and gesture at the house behind him, and despite her empathy for Michael, she found herself moved by Drew's intentions for this place. This was no publicity stunt. He had ambitious plans for the children this center would serve, and the enthusiasm in his voice when he spoke about them was genuine.

"Here at the Kingston Youth Center, we hope to make dreams a very real part of kids' lives. With your help, we plan to offer programs that support underprivileged children's success in academics, sports, and the arts. We hope to send the message that where you start in life doesn't determine where you finish, and that the only limits out there are the ones we place on ourselves."

His words captured Shannon's attention. Limits. She was painfully familiar with them. Would she have grown up to be a very different person if someone had fostered such sentiments in her when she was a struggling child? Would limits have had any hold on her like they seemed to now?

Drew accepted a pair of large ceremonial scissors from a smiling city councilmember standing off to the side. "Without further ado, I give you the Kingston Youth Center." He cut the ribbon in two, and the cut ends drifted gracefully to the ground.

The crowd applauded once more and cheered. Camera flashes went off everywhere.

Shannon merely watched silently, Drew's words echoing in her head.

• • •

Drew's speech was still on Shannon's mind as she washed dishes in her kitchen sink that evening, staring unseeingly out the window and into the darkness of her backyard.

Where you start in life doesn't determine where you finish.

It was hardly the message she had heard from her parents while growing up, content as they were to go on living hand to mouth without ever trying to change their circumstances. And she certainly hadn't heard it from her peers, either. Quite the opposite. But she had dared to reach a *little* beyond their expectations, hadn't she? Maybe night school wasn't glamorous, but she had earned a degree. *And* made a home for herself. And she liked to think she made a difference at work, too. More of a difference than anyone else in her family ever had, at least.

Dropping the dishcloth in the sink, Shannon turned around and leaned back against the counter to let her eyes roam over the kitchen she had remodeled all by herself, and not too shabbily at that.

Limits, she thought again. They hadn't held her back anywhere else in her life, just in personal matters, but they had crippled her there. Years of believing she wasn't good enough, or desirable enough, to warrant a man's affection. So she had played it safe by remaining on the sidelines where ridicule and rejection couldn't reach her.

And what had that gotten her? Ten years of pining after the same man, all without him ever having a clue about her feelings. Ten years of loneliness and waiting for something to happen. She had gotten very good at waiting. Maybe too good.

What if ...

Old doubts surged up before she could even finish the thought, but she pushed past them.

What if she got off the sidelines, just this once, and went to see Michael? What if she stopped watching everyone else play the game and actually made a move herself?

He won't want you, her inner voice whispered knowingly.

That was certainly possible. Her heart rate sped up just at the thought of daring to tell Michael about her feelings for him, and sudden nausea made her stomach turn over. He wouldn't mock her, she was sure. But he might pity her, and the thought of that made her heart pound all over again. She wasn't sure she could bear pity from him.

Well, she would be safe from pity if she stayed home, all right. But something else nagged at her besides that cruel inner voice, something that suggested if she didn't do something to break the pattern of old habits now, then she never would.

Bo came trotting into the kitchen, and Shannon bent down to run her fingers through his soft fur. He licked her nose, and she cradled his muzzle in her hands to look him in the eyes.

"I've got to do it, don't I?" she whispered out loud, and the words hung in the air. "I've got to go tell him. If I don't..." She trailed off, picturing herself in another ten years, still living exactly the same life as she was now with all her inhibitions and insecurities. The loneliness of it unsettled her as much as the idea of exposing her feelings to Michael.

Bo cocked his ears at the sound of her voice and whined as if he picked up on the tension in it.

Shannon sank down onto the floor and pulled Bo onto her lap, even though he was much too big to be a lapdog. He didn't seem to mind, though, and even redoubled his efforts to lick her face. She wrapped her arms around him and hugged him tightly as if doing so might somehow give her courage.

It didn't work, but she came to her decision anyway.

She would go. And she would tell him. For better or for worse, she would tell him.

If she didn't throw up first.

Chapter Twelve

"Clarissa? I need a favor." Shannon cradled the phone between her shoulder and her chin as her hands busied themselves in packing a small overnight bag. "I'm sorry to call you so late in the evening, but—"

"It's fine, honey, it's not that late." There was concern in Clarissa's voice. "Is everything okay?"

"Yeah, it's just—I need to go out of town. Just for a day or two, maybe, but I'll need you to cover Drew's phone for me."

"Absolutely. So a trip? Not a bad idea. Might be the best thing to lift your spirits. May I ask where you're going, or am I being too nosy?"

Shannon hesitated before answering, suspecting her friend would disapprove of her answer. The disapproval part didn't bother her, it was the attempt to talk her out of going that no doubt would follow. "To see Michael," she said finally.

There was silence on the other end.

"Hello?" Shannon asked, wary.

"I'm here," Clarissa returned somberly.

"You think I'm nuts."

"Not nuts, just—oh, Shannon, are you sure this is wise?"

Shannon let out a rueful little laugh. "No. I'm really not."

"Then why do it? There are plenty of nice men here in town, men who are stable and well-rounded and everything you could ever want."

"I want *him*."

Clarissa's frown was practically audible. "Why? Because he's handsome?"

"Because I like who I am when I'm with him." Shannon stared at the wall before her, seeing Michael's face instead and the way he had looked at her that night at the football field. "And I think maybe he could feel the same way about me." She felt a flicker of warmth at the memory, and hope.

"I suspect a lot of women have liked the way he made them feel when they were with him, Shannon. Until the morning after, at least. I just don't want to see you end up as another notch on his bedpost."

Heat rushed into Shannon's cheeks. "Clarissa! That's not why I'm going to see him."

"Maybe not, but what happens when you actually do see him again? You might do something you'll regret—"

"I already have," Shannon burst out.

"What? Oh, honey," Clarissa said with obvious dismay.

"Not *that*," Shannon returned, feeling the heat in her face grow. "What I meant is I regret the way I've spent the last ten years of my life, Clarissa. Ten years just waiting and hoping. Ten years I'll never get back."

Her friend was silent.

"I don't want to live like that anymore. I feel like I've lost so much time as it is, and life's just too short to waste chances like that."

"I don't want to see you get hurt, Shannon."

"I know. And I appreciate that," Shannon said softly. Then she let out a breath that was half-sigh, half-laugh, but it was without mirth. "Hey, cheer up. Chances are he'll give me a platonic little pat on the head and just send me on my way, and all this worry will have been for nothing." Her heart hurt at the thought, but she kept her voice carefully neutral.

Or maybe she didn't, because Clarissa's voice turned gentle. "You've never given yourself enough credit, honey. You're a warm, wonderful, and *lovely* young woman, and no man in his right mind is just going to send you on your way. That's what worries me."

"He wouldn't use me like that." That was one thing of which she did feel sure. "He might not want me, but he wouldn't treat me the way you're afraid he might."

"Maybe you're right, but he's not the kind of man a woman settles down with, Shannon. Or builds a future with."

"Could be." Shannon swallowed hard, her mouth dry. "But I guess there's only one way to find out."

There was a long pause before Clarissa spoke again. "I'm not going to be able to talk you out of this, am I?"

"No."

The older woman sighed. "Then I suppose there's nothing left to say except I'm here if you need me. "

As in, to pick up the pieces, Shannon thought with a pang. "Could you maybe look in on Bo while I'm gone?"

"Sure, honey."

Shannon drew a deep breath. "Clarissa?"

"Yes?"

Her voice shook. "I'm kind of terrified."

"Honey, you've got more guts than you realize. Regardless of what happens with Michael, remember that, okay?"

"I'll try. Thanks."

"And if you change your mind, there's a nice young man who works at the drugstore that I could—"

"Clarissa." But Shannon's mouth curved upward.

"All right, all right." There was a pause. "Call me when you get back."

"I will."

Shannon hung up the phone and stared at the overnight bag in front of her. "Well," she said aloud. "Here goes nothing."

•••

After yet another restless night of tossing and turning, Shannon dragged herself out of bed as soon as the light of dawn glowed outside her window. Might as well get an early start and get this over with that much sooner, she supposed. She wasn't going to get any more sleep this morning anyway. But determined as she was to see this whole thing through with Michael, her anxiety made her movements slow as she dressed.

Even choosing clothes to wear had proven stressful, as if success depended on the right style of shirt or accessories. Stop it, she told herself, and then simply grabbed the first plain T-shirt she saw in her bureau drawer along with a pair of jeans. Michael knew she was no glamour girl. If it turned out he did want her, then the clothes shouldn't matter.

Shannon started to put her hair in its usual braid and then caught sight of her reflection in the dresser mirror. She slowly let her hands fall away from her hair, and its fiery waves hung freely past her shoulders. Vibrancy and color, that was what Clarissa had said. Would Shannon herself ever be able to see it that way? It was hard to imagine such a thing. Taunts from her childhood filled her memory, and her hands twitched as if barely resisting the urge to twist the strands tightly back into old familiar confines. There was safety in hiding, after all.

Your hair is beautiful.

She heard Michael's voice in her head and closed her eyes. Enough hiding. She was not a child anymore, or an insecure teenager. It was high time she let the past go, even if she wasn't entirely sure yet how to do that. Little by little, she decided. Starting now.

She left her hair down and went downstairs to feed Bo his breakfast.

A few minutes later, she was in her car with her key in the ignition. Don't you dare look back, she told herself, and she pulled the car out of the driveway and headed for the highway before she could change her mind.

• • •

The internet was an amazing thing. So were smartphones, Shannon thought, pulling her car into the parking lot of the bar that the directions on her phone swore belonged to Michael.

Even though it was getting dark out, it was easy to see the lot was over half full, and Shannon could see enough inside the windows to tell the bar was far from empty. Fantastic. So she would have an audience to her reunion with Michael, at least at first. *Couldn't be easy, could it?*

Her knuckles were white on the steering wheel. She peeled them off it and cut the engine but stayed put in the car, her eyes on the building. Through its windows she caught glimpses of people laughing and clinking glasses together, their movements casual and relaxed, in complete contrast with the turmoil inside of her. What else was new? She'd have thought she'd gotten used to being the odd one out by now.

Shannon forced herself to open the car door and step out. Closing the door behind her, she leaned against it for support and took a deep breath. Maybe he won't even be there tonight, she thought with a mixture of dread and hope.

But then she caught sight of him through one of the front windows, and her panicky heart beat even faster. He was delivering a handful of drinks to a group of women who were obviously ogling him, giggling behind their hands and fluttering eyelashes that looked much too long to be real. One of them, a blonde, tossed her hair and laughed at something Michael said.

Shannon's eyes widened, and she abruptly turned to open the car door again, intending to leap back inside. At the last second, she managed to stop herself.

No. She had already decided there was no going back, and she meant it. It wasn't really so complicated, was it? All she had to do was walk up to him and be honest about her feelings. If he didn't feel the same way about her, they could still shake hands and part friends. And she could walk away with her dignity intact and her head held high.

Sure, if this was an after-school special, Shannon thought, her mouth going dry. Real life never seemed to be that simple.

But she pushed off from the car with her hands and began walking toward the entrance of the bar with her feet dragging like a prisoner on the way to her execution. Her palms were so sweaty they nearly slipped off the handle of the door when she reached it. Wiping them on her jeans, she tried again and stepped inside.

• • •

Michael's latest customers were living it up and painting the town tonight judging by the shortness of their skirts and the hints of glam from head to toe. And by the way they let their eyes roam over him as he approached with their drinks, they were looking for company of the male variety. He wished now that he had sent Sammy out with their drinks instead.

Michael set each drink in front of its respective owner, pretending he didn't notice the looks they were giving him. "Margarita, gin and tonic, house ale, and club soda with a twist of lime," he finished, sliding it before an attractive blonde who had an air of authority about her and was likely the ringleader of the group.

The blonde shook her head and switched the drinks. "That's hers," she corrected him with a coy smile and a nod of her head to one of her companions. "She's the designated driver. Unless, of course—" Here she leaned closer to Michael, "someone else winds up taking me home tonight."

Her friends giggled into their drinks.

Michael gave the blonde a polite but indifferent smile. "Not your first round of drinks tonight, is it, ladies?"

There were more smirks and appraising glances.

Michael subtly extracted his arm from the grasp of one of the four giggly women and took a step back and out of their reach. "Enjoy your drinks," he said politely, and then he turned around to head back to the bar —

And froze as brilliant coppery hair caught his eye and he met Shannon's gaze where she stood just inside the doorway.

She lifted one hand in a half-hearted flicker of a wave, her expression uncertain and uneasy.

Michael blinked at her in shock and might have stood there staring even longer if a passing customer hadn't bumped into him and jolted him back to awareness. Finding his voice at last, he wound his way around a couple of tables and stopped in front of her. "Shannon?" Her unexpected presence there sent a wave of pure pleasure through him so sharp it was almost painful.

She shoved her hands into the front pockets of her jeans and dropped her eyes to his chest. "Hi."

Her hair was down around her shoulders, which reminded him immediately of the evening they spent together in the high school parking lot. And of the kiss before that. His pulse grew erratic. "Why—what are you doing here?"

Her eyes darted up to meet his briefly, then dropped again. "I, uh…there's something I need to—I mean—"

A group of happy customers a few tables over erupted in hoots and guffaws at something one of them did, and whatever else

Shannon said was drowned out. Michael bent closer to try and hear her. "What?"

She took a deep breath. "I said—"

But more noise interrupted her. "Here," Michael said, putting a hand on the small of her back to steer her toward the back room. "Come with me."

She jumped at the contact, and Michael quickly let his hand fall away from her. He gestured ahead instead, and she moved in that direction. His eyes followed her every movement even as he followed her: the way she kept nervously brushing her hair back behind one ear, the way each step drew his attention to the natural motion of her hips…He tore his eyes away from them a second before she glanced furtively over her shoulder at him.

What was she doing here?

Michael closed the door behind them once they were inside the makeshift office, shutting out the noise of the bar. The size of the room made it impossible to put much space between the two of them, so he remained by the door while Shannon hovered by the wall farthest from him. She seemed tense, and he racked his brain trying to figure out what reason she might have for tracking him down like this instead of simply calling. It would have to be something important, something —

He stiffened. "Did something happen? Is Drew okay?"

Shannon turned away from the wall to face him. Sort of. Her eyes looked everywhere but at his, and her hands remained rigidly in her pockets. "Drew's fine. Everything's fine."

"Oh," he said with relief but also confusion. He was back to square one then. "Okay. I just figured…I'm just surprised to see you here."

"Yeah," she acknowledged, her voice strained. "I Googled you, and…" She swallowed hard as if her mouth had grown suddenly dry. "Nice place."

"Thanks. Small business, backbone of America, right?"

She made a noncommittal sort of sound, and then she began biting her bottom lip. His eyes fixated on that tiny action, and an image of him sweeping his desk clear and bringing her down on top of it suddenly flickered into his mind. He forced it out again and crossed his arms over his chest in an attempt to keep his hands out of trouble.

Shannon leaned back against the wall as if for support. "So," she said finally. "The dedication ceremony was yesterday."

Michael nodded grimly.

"It was nice. It's going to be a good place, Michael. Your parents would like it."

"I hope you're right."

She scuffed at some invisible mark on the floor with the toe of her shoe. "Drew gave a good speech," she continued softly.

"I'm sure he did." A new image popped into his head then, one of his brother and Shannon at the ceremony. Had their eyes met during his speech? Had they exchanged special smiles meant only for each other? Michael's stomach turned suddenly queasy, and he mentally berated himself. Who was he to get jealous and possessive? She was with the man she should be with, and it was for the best. But the words just seemed to refuse to sink in no matter how many times he repeated them in his head. Just a few more minutes, he told himself. Just a few more minutes of hanging on to whatever slim bit of his resolve remained, and then she would say whatever she had come to say and leave. He could fake nonchalance for a little longer, couldn't he? He forced a smile onto his face and spoke with false cheerfulness. "So, you two—"

She shook her head. "No."

That single word sent a sudden rush of pleasure and relief through him, and he was grateful her eyes remained downcast so he had time to wipe those feelings from his expression before she could see them. *Bastard. Don't you want her to be happy?* "You aren't? Why not?"

Then she finally did look up at him, and her eyes were filled with what he had fantasized about seeing there since the day he said goodbye to her on her deck. Her eyes were filled with him.

Oh, hell, he thought with despair.

• • •

Shannon held Michael's gaze long enough to see his eyes widen with realization, and then she was forced to look down again, too overwhelmed by her nerves to maintain eye contact. All in all, this was actually going better than she had expected. She hadn't thrown up yet, or passed out. And it looked like she didn't have to worry about finding the right words to tell him anymore, which was good since none of the speeches she had considered during the drive here belonged anywhere outside of a soap opera. But it would be nice if he would say something.

Anything.

"Shannon..." he said finally, his voice faltering and strained.

She shrugged without looking up and managed a shaky laugh even though her insides were churning. "Yeah, I know. Go figure, huh?"

"Sweetheart, you—this is a mistake. You're just confused."

She swallowed again and made herself look him in the eye. "I'm not confused."

His own eyes were still wide, and much of the color had drained from his face. "Yes, you are," he insisted, his jaw twitching. "Drew's the one you want. He's what you've wanted since high school, right? You said so yourself."

"I was wrong."

"No, you weren't. Drew's the good brother. He's grounded, he's dependable, he's—"

"He's not the one I want," she said softly, her heart pounding. If she thrust her hands any deeper into her pockets, she'd put holes in them.

Michael ran his hands through his hair and started pacing, difficult to do in a room this small. Her attention followed him as she tried to interpret his reaction. Well, it wasn't pity at least. She was sure of that. Unfortunately, it didn't look a whole lot like the rapture of a man in love, either, she thought with a sinking feeling.

"Damn it, this is all my fault," he muttered more to himself than to her, his expression one of obvious distress.

Shannon blinked, startled. She had imagined this conversation taking many different turns, but this was not one of them. "I beg your pardon?"

"It was the kiss, wasn't it? That night at the park. I should never have kissed you. I shouldn't have—damn it, I got your head all mixed up, that's all. Don't you see that?"

"What?"

He swore under his breath. "You were doing just fine before I came along."

"Not really, I wasn't."

"Well you were seeing things a lot more clearly than you are now. I just…" Michael shook his head and stopped pacing only to slump back against the door, looking for all the world like he'd been given the worst news of life.

In the midst of all the stomach-turning emotions going on inside her, Shannon felt a flicker of irritation. What did he have to get so upset about? She was the one going out on a limb here, after all, not him. "You just what?"

"I…" He gestured helplessly. "You don't really want me. Trust me."

"I don't really want you," she repeated slowly. Her tone got cooler, but he didn't seem to notice.

"No, you don't. You just *think* you do, because—"

"Because…you dazzled me?" Her irritation grew, loosening her tongue. Did *everyone* believe she was an impressionable idiot?

"Maybe. I don't know." He sighed. "I mean, you were inexperienced—"

"Inexperienced, sure. Not stupid!"

Michael looked up at her, startled, and took a hesitant step toward her as if to calm her down. "Shannon—"

"Oh, shut up!" She yanked her hands out of her pockets and gave him a shove in the middle of his chest that sent him staggering back against the door. "You jerk! You really think you're 'all that,' don't you?"

If possible, his eyes grew even wider. "No, it's just—" He tried again to go to her.

She shoved him away again. "You really think I'm such a bumpkin all you had to do was smile and I'd be swept off my feet? I'm such a wallflower that's all it would take? Are you really that full of yourself?" She glared at him as he stared at her, speechless. "Well? Say something!"

"No, I'm not full of myself. It's just…"

"What? It's just what?" she demanded.

Michael cleared his throat. "It's just that it *has* happened to me a few times before," he said awkwardly.

Oh.

She felt a little of the wind go out of her sails as she realized it was no doubt true. Women had been throwing themselves at his feet for years because of his looks. Why wouldn't he assume she'd do the same?

Her eyes narrowed. Because he ought to have known her better than that, that's why. Her temper rekindled. He thought she was just like the rest of them.

She opened her mouth to reiterate what a jerk he was, but then stopped as she noticed the shadows under his eyes and the misery all over his face.

He thought she was just like the rest of them.

That would have hurt more except she had a sneaking suspicion it had less to do with his opinion of her than it did with his opinion of himself. He didn't think he had anything to offer a woman besides sex appeal. *No one in high school knew the real me*—wasn't that what he said before? He was a good time, and that was it.

Her anger softened somewhat, and she took a step toward him. "Michael—"

He frowned warily. "Are you going to plant me into the wall again?"

"What? No—" None of this was going at all the way she planned. She gave up trying to figure it all out and blurted out the first thing that came to mind. "You think I don't really know you, don't you?"

He stared at her, and she thought she saw some of his guardedness drop away. For a moment, at least. "You probably know me better than anyone has in a long time," he countered quietly. "But—"

"But not well enough to see past your face, is that it? Past your looks and charm?"

"There's not much else to see."

"Yes, there is. You're loyal, and kind, and—"

He shook his head. "You're just seeing what you want to see, Shannon. I—"

"Oh, for crying out loud," she exclaimed, her frustration growing again. "You actually think I'm too blind see who you really are? That I couldn't possibly feel anything real for you?"

Michael's face was unreadable, but he didn't interrupt her this time. In fact, he almost seemed to be holding his breath as he waited for her to continue.

"Well, I'm not blind. I see your faults just fine. Want me to prove it?" She started ticking them off on her fingers as she listed them. "For starters, you're a little vain. And you rely on your looks to get what you want way too much. And you're too hung up on the past, too." She paused for a minute to pull together her scattered thoughts. "You don't think things through all that well, and you're headstrong—and it's not like you're *that* good-looking, you know," she added, sounding a little sullen even to her own ears.

Good grief. Shakespeare she was not.

She shut her mouth abruptly, thinking that if this even remotely qualified as a declaration of love, it had to be the worst one in the history of mankind.

"I see," Michael said gravely after a minute of awkward silence. "Thank you for your honesty."

"You're welcome," she said stiffly.

He ran a hand over his mouth as if he was trying not to smile, and something in his heavy manner softened. "So, you drove all this way to tell me how screwed up I am and that you don't really find me very attractive?"

Shannon could feel her cheeks bloom with heat. "Well, that wasn't my original plan, no." She took a deep breath. "Look, I don't know if you want me or not, but—"

"Sweetheart, you have no idea."

She let her breath out with a slight hitch and a rush of emotion. "Then why did you leave? And what was all this," she waved her hand at the room around them, "tonight?"

"I was trying to be noble and self-sacrificing."

"Well, knock it off!"

Michael started to laugh, and it was a sound that was full of relief. "Yes, ma'am," he said obediently, and then in about two seconds he closed the short distance remaining between them to take Shannon's startled face between his hands and bring his mouth to hers.

Recovering from her surprise, Shannon wrapped her arms around his neck and held on for dear life as heat rushed through her. Her fingers curled in his hair, and his hands travelled slowly down her back, making her heart pound even faster. So the night at the park had not been a fluke, she realized, feeling lightheaded. The lips this man had, and the things that he could do with them …

But this time she was not the only one affected by it, because Michael seemed out of breath, too, when they finally separated—and he did not go far. He touched her face with his fingers, and then ran them through her hair as he looked at her searchingly. "You sure about this?" he asked her softly, and the tentative look in his eyes made her want to wrap her arms around him all the more.

She nodded, unable to speak so soon after the way he had just kissed her.

"I'm pretty screwed up, you know. I'm not sure I'm worth the—"

Shannon shut him up with another kiss, her feelings for him overcoming her shyness, and any hesitation that might have plagued Michael seemed to vanish then because all Shannon knew after that was that his lips and his hands seemed to be everywhere at once. And yet somehow it still didn't feel like enough of him.

"I hated the idea of my brother doing this with you," he said finally against her mouth. "It drove me crazy."

His words sent a little thrill down her spine. "Really?" she managed, her voice somewhat breathless but not so breathless that she couldn't hear the undercurrent of delight in it. She was sure Michael must have heard it, too.

"Yeah," he said, his lips traveling over her jaw and down to her throat. "And this…"

Her skin felt like it was on fire wherever he touched it. "Anything else?" she asked him, wishing her voice didn't tremble quite so much but glad she had gotten it working again.

"Oh, yes," he whispered against her neck, and she could hear the smile in his voice. "Let me show you…"

Epilogue

Two months later

She was as ready as she was ever going to be for this night.

Shannon examined her reflection in the mirror in her bedroom, twisting this way and that to make sure there weren't any wrinkles or loose threads that needed attention—or worse, any part of her skirt accidentally tucked into her pantyhose.

Nope. Everything appeared to be as it should be. Including her hair, which she deliberately left down. It was getting easier to do that now, and if she wasn't exactly a full-fledged woman of confidence yet, she liked to think she was making strides in that direction.

Despite its lack of wrinkles, she smoothed the dress's silky jade green fabric anyway, more out of nerves than anything else. It was a pretty dress—"It is now," Michael had said when she tried it on for him for the first time. He had then tried very hard to coax her into slipping back out of it.

She smiled now at the memory. It gave her a little boost of confidence, which she sorely needed tonight.

Her ten-year reunion. She had been dreading it since she first got the invitation in the mail weeks ago, which was one reason why she was making herself go. It was ridiculous, she had decided, that one single social event should strike fear into anybody's heart like this, particularly if that person was no longer an insecure teenager.

So she was going. But she had lost count of the number of times she had nearly blurted it out to Michael and asked him to go as her date. It would have been a lot less intimidating—and, quite honestly, kind of fantastic—to walk into a room full of her former classmates on the arm of the heartthrob of their high school years, but he'd spent years being treated as little more than eye candy. She was not about to treat him that way, too.

Besides, it was better this way, she told herself. More fitting. It meant she wasn't afraid to stand on her own two feet around the people who used to intimidate the crud out of her, right?

Right. It sounded good anyway, even if her subconscious wasn't buying it.

It wasn't as if she would be totally without allies there, she reminded herself as she gave Bo a pat on the head and collected her purse. Drew would be there, too, and now that she wasn't tongue-tied around him anymore they were genuinely becoming friends. He was even softening toward his brother, which Shannon knew was no small thing to Michael.

So even if she was going stag tonight, it was comforting to know that she could at least count on a dance or two with the former prom king and student body president of the McKinley High class of 2003.

Going downstairs, Shannon grabbed a sweater from the hall closet and opened the front door.

And saw Michael reclining against the porch railing, dressed to the nines in black slacks and a dress shirt that was missing a tie and open at the collar but still somehow amazingly dashing on him.

She stared at him in shock while his eyes travelled over her appreciatively, and he smiled in greeting. "Wow," he murmured in a voice that sent delicious shivers down her spine. "You look like every man's fantasy come true." He straightened and came over to where she still stood speechless, then bent to kiss her, slowly and very deliberately.

She blinked at him when he finally separated his lips from hers.

"So, are you ready then?" he asked her, offering her his arm.

"I—what?"

"Are you ready to go?" Michael checked his watch. "Doors open at eight, right?"

"What doors?"

"At the high school. It is eight, isn't it?"

"How did you know…" She trailed off, confused as to what he was doing there. Delighted, but confused.

"Drew told me. Or did you forget that he and I are on speaking terms now?"

"*Drew* told you?" That would teach her to confide in her boss.

"Yes, he did. He also told me why you neglected to mention it to me." Michael's voice softened along with the light in his eyes as he looked into hers.

"Oh." Yes, she was really going to have to think twice before spilling anything to Drew again, or at least anything more personal than her grocery list, she thought as she felt her cheeks grow warm. "Well…"

"You're very sweet, you know that?"

Her cheeks grew even warmer.

"And I appreciate you trying to protect my feelings," he continued, with a solemn look but a suspicious twinkle in his dark eyes. "But I'm afraid you're just going to have to get used to being seen in public with me."

"Well, if I have to, I have to," she conceded gravely, and then she grinned and put her arms around him. "Thanks for coming tonight. I was dreading going alone."

"Wouldn't miss it. Although—" He trailed his fingers down her back. "I wouldn't mind cutting out early."

Yes, early was good, she thought with another lovely shiver as his fingers left a trail of heat on her skin. Then she took the arm he offered her and followed him off the porch.

He stopped halfway to his truck and turned to look at her in the deepening twilight. "Shannon…" he started, and this time his voice was soft and halting. "I—"

"Yes?"

"You and me, we…"

She held her breath. The look in his eyes was so earnest, it made her heart do a funny sort of flip inside her chest. He almost seemed, well, *shy*. Michael Kingston, heartbreaker, was clearly struggling to say something he wasn't used to saying to a woman, and his awkwardness at that moment was all the more endearing for that. "Yes?" she said again, more softly.

"I've never—I mean…" He cleared his throat and tried again, the rising color in his cheeks obvious even in the growing darkness. "I just want to say…I…"

"Yeah," she told him, her heart thumping pleasantly fast. "Me, too."

"I—yeah?"

"Yeah."

Michael took a deep breath. "Well, good. I'm glad we had this talk…" And he drew her toward him. She went quite willingly.

Several minutes later, Shannon tore her mouth away from his. "We're going to be late," she told him breathlessly.

"So then we just get to make more of an entrance—"

She laughed and pulled him in the direction of his truck. "Come on. I promised myself I'd go to this thing, and I meant it."

He sighed but gave in and followed her. "I guess it would be a shame to waste the sight of you in that dress. You're going to outshine everybody else there."

"Flattery will get you nowhere."

Michael opened the passenger's side door for her. "Nowhere?"

"Well maybe somewhere," she admitted. "But I need to get to this reunion before I lose my nerve, so—"

"Understood." He closed the door after her and then rounded the truck to get in on the driver's side. "It might actually be fun, you know. Seeing old faces, catching up on what people have been doing for the past ten years…"

"Uh huh. Sure."

"Hey, keep an open mind."

"Catching up shouldn't take long. Not much has happened to me in the last decade."

He turned the key in the ignition. "Wait until your next reunion. You'll have all sorts of news to tell people then."

"Will I?"

"Oh, yeah," he told her, giving her a look that was full of promise. "I guarantee it."

More from This Author

(From *Coming Home*)

"Girl, you're lookin' better than a body has a right to."

Callie didn't look up from the notepad she was scribbling in. "I'm all for recycling, Kalvin, but you've used that line one too many times within my earshot for it to work on me."

"Ah, baby, but you're the only one I ever really meant it with."

"Mmm." She kept writing and ignored the teenager's insincere protests of love. He had wandered into the store a few weeks ago, spotted her, and then found an excuse to return almost every afternoon. Points for persistence, she thought.

It was a lazy and very hot afternoon at Vintage Records Your Way, and Callie had little to do behind the counter except write, which was the main reason why she took the job in the first place four months ago. Other than Kalvin, the only other people in the store seemed to be browsing through the merchandise merely as an excuse to avoid the intense heat radiating off the New York City pavement, and that was fine with her. The job was enough to help her make rent, once it was split three ways among Callie and her two roommates. Her boss might be a jerk, but she'd managed to save up enough money to be moving along soon anyway. And the music was good, too. She cocked her head slightly to better hear the strains of Janis Joplin coming over the store sound system and closed her eyes, pencil poised above her paper as she waited for inspiration.

She got more of Kalvin instead.

"Come on, aren't you ever going to go out with me?"

She shook her head.

"Why not?"

"I wouldn't want to ruin the friendship," she said dryly, raising one eyebrow.

"Well, it's not like we're *close* friends…"

Giving up on her writing for the moment, she looked at him with fond exasperation. He grinned at her hopefully. The expression was rather adorable on his gawky, young face, and she suspected that he knew it. "Kalvin, why don't you go hit on that girl over there? The one in the pink skirt who's trying to pretend she knows who Blue Oyster Cult is. She's cute, and she's your own age," she added pointedly.

He shrugged and leaned on the counter with his elbows. "Already tried. Struck out."

Callie let out an incredulous laugh. "So I'm your sloppy seconds?"

"Technically," he corrected her with one finger raised in the air, "I think the term 'sloppy seconds' would mean that you were passed on to me after some other guy had you. Which I'm fine with, by the way."

"That's so open-minded of you. Go away now, please, so I can concentrate." She bent over the notebook again.

He strained to see what she was writing. "What are you working on this time? Politics? The environment? Sex and the single girl?"

Suddenly self-conscious, she flipped the notebook over before he could read anything. "It's personal this time, Kalvin."

"Oooh. Like a diary? Going to send it off to *Cosmo* when you're finished?"

But she only waved him off with one hand and scooted her stool back further from the counter so she could write in peace. Grumbling under his breath, Kalvin finally wandered away to give the girl in the pink skirt another try. When Callie was sure he was safely away, she turned her notebook over again and reread what she had already written:

After a while, you start to doubt yourself, to wonder if—on some level—you're looking for him in every man you meet. Looking for his approval. Looking for answers. And it doesn't matter if it's a passing acquaintance or someone who is more of a permanent fixture in your life. You begin to wonder if you're hoping that this time, you'll get it right. Or maybe that this time he'll get it right.

She frowned. It was more wistful than she'd originally intended, which she found vaguely unsettling. This was supposed to be a more clinical piece to submit to a particular journal, a reflection on the effects of absent fathers. They would never accept it this way. Flipping over to a fresh, empty page, she touched her pencil to the paper to try again.

The phone rang then, interrupting her, and she reached absentmindedly for the receiver. "Vintage Records Your Way. What can I do for you?"

"Callie? Oh, good, it's you. This is Tina."

Callie blinked in surprise. It was the more unreliable one of her two roommates. She wasn't very close to either one of them, really. They kept very different hours and rarely crossed paths, and the only other time Tina had called Callie at work was when a pipe had burst in their apartment. A prickle of dread crept down her neck, and she tried to keep the wariness out of her voice. "Tina? What's up?"

"You got a phone call a few minutes ago on the landline, and—look, is there someone else there who can finish your shift for you or something?"

Callie's tension grew. "Manager's in the back. Why?"

"There's been an accident. Your mom's in the hospital."

"What?" she asked sharply, jerking up from the stool and dropping her notebook on the floor. "What kind of accident? Is she all right?"

Hospital. Memories came rushing back at the mere mention of the word. The cop on their doorstep, silhouetted in the night by his patrol car's headlights. Liddy's terror as they rushed into the ER. And Elliot ...

Eight years ago, and the loss of her brother still felt fresh. It seemed cruel, somehow, that fate would not allow the details of that night to dim from her memory.

"She fell off a ladder or something and broke her leg, I think," Tina said. "I'm not sure of all the details. Guy just said she fell, broke something, and she's in the hospital. Said she should be okay, but asked if you could fly out there."

"That's all you can tell me?"

"Sorry. I'm going on about three hours of sleep here. I wasn't at my sharpest."

Tina worked the night shift at a twenty-four hour bagel shop, which was one reason why she and Callie didn't cross paths much.

"But you're sure he said she was going to be okay, right?"

"Sounded that way, yeah. But he did seem pretty serious, too."

Taking a deep breath, Callie bit back a frustrated response. "Who was it who called?"

There was silence on the other end of the line as her sleep-deprived roommate struggled to remember. "Danny," she said finally. "I think his name was Danny."

An image of him blossomed in her mind, and her pulse quickened. Sandy brown curls, damp as they so often were after a day spent on the river with Elliot. Skin tanned to a warm shade of caramel after a summer in the sun. Strong, lean. And eyes that had captured her then teenage heart the first time she looked into them ...

She closed her eyes and willed the image away before it could melt her any further.

Danny. How long had it been since she'd heard that name? He must have gotten her phone number from her mother because the last time she'd spoken to him herself was long before she came to

New York. And even her mother didn't have her new cell phone number. She felt a twinge of guilt. "Did he leave a number?"

"Sorry. Couldn't find a pencil. Don't worry, though, Cal. Caller ID." Her roommate paused for a moment. Let's see... McCutcheon. Is that him?"

"Yes." Amid the turmoil caused by the mention of his name, she felt at least some measure of relief. If Danny said Liddy would be okay, then Liddy would be okay. Then again, Tina's recollection of his exact words couldn't necessarily be counted on to be accurate. And she *had* said he sounded serious. Liddy was not exactly a young woman, and there could be complications with even the smallest of accidents. Callie bent to retrieve her notebook and quickly jotted down the number Tina read her. "I'll be home as soon I can," she said. "You can go back to sleep now."

"Okay." There was a poorly stifled yawn on the other end of the line. "Sorry about your mom."

"Thanks."

Callie dropped the receiver in its place, snatched up her notebook, and grabbed her purse from where it lay behind the counter. Ignoring the curious looks of some of the customers, she pushed open a door marked "Employees Only" and met the startled gaze of her manager, Les. He was a balding skeleton of a man who wore his hair extra long on the sides to make up for the lack of it on top. He was also lazy, a grouch, and a bully.

"What the—who's manning the counter?" he demanded irritably, looking up from the pages of a skin magazine.

"You are," she informed him, looping her purse strap over her shoulder. "I've got a family emergency, and I'm going to need to leave town for a while."

Setting the magazine aside, he folded his long, skinny arms over his chest. "What kind of emergency?"

"My mom had an accident."

"She going to be okay?"

"Probably, but—"

Scowling, he picked up his magazine again. "Then what's the emergency? Forget it. You can't just walk out on such short notice. The schedule's already made for next week. Maybe go the week after."

"I wasn't asking your permission."

His eyes narrowed. "What did you just say to me?"

"I said I'm going to see my mom. I thought a little time off would do it, but a permanent arrangement works just fine, too, you little pissant."

She tossed her copy of the store key at him and walked out as he scrambled to catch it. As she strode toward the front door, she nearly ran down Kalvin.

"What happened?" he asked, wide-eyed.

"A little managerial dispute. Long story short, there's a job opening here if you're interested, kiddo." She gave his arm a quick, affectionate squeeze and let the front door swing shut behind her.

Callie's days there had been numbered anyway. At four months, it was one of the longer jobs she had held, and she was beginning to get that familiar flicker of restlessness that told her it was time to move on. She knew it wouldn't be hard for Les to find a replacement for her. He just didn't like to put down his magazines long enough to conduct any interviews.

Pausing in the sweltering heat, she took a deep breath and dialed the number Tina had given her. It went to voicemail. She wasn't sure if she was relieved or disappointed.

"You've reached Danny McCutcheon's voicemail. You know what to do."

It was a short recording, but it was enough to make her pulse speed up. His voice was casual in the message, warm and mellow. Very different from the last time she'd heard it. She stood there in the middle of the sidewalk with her mouth open, rattled and unable to think of anything to say. Abruptly, she ended the call. Forget it. She'd try again later.

She used the walk home to search online for flights with her cell phone, and by the time she got to her apartment building, she already had a red-eye flight lined up for that evening. There was no boyfriend to say goodbye to and no pets to worry about, not even a potted plant that would need watering. That was the great thing about being a nomad, Callie thought as she threw some clothes into a bag. No strings to tie you down or hold you back.

• • •

Between packing and dealing with the usual chaos at the airport that happened with a last minute flight, Callie found plenty of excuses to put off trying to reach Danny again. At least for a few hours. But finally, as she settled into a seat near her gate of departure, she fingered the phone in her hand before slowly and reluctantly dialing his number.

Voicemail again. She let out the breath she hadn't realized she was holding and cleared her throat, determined to speak this time.

"Danny? It's Callie. I'm at JFK right now, and my flight leaves in about twenty minutes. I'll have a few layovers, but I should be in Portland by about 10:30 tomorrow morning, coming in from San Francisco." She glanced at her watch. It read 12:02. No wonder she was so tired. "I mean, 10:30 *this* morning, I guess. I'll rent a car or get a cab; I haven't figured that part out yet. Hopefully I'll be at the hospital no later than noon." She paused, feeling that she ought to say something more but struggling to think of the right words. He deserved more than simple pleasantries from her, but she couldn't bring herself to say anything too personal without opening doors best left closed. "Thanks for calling me, Danny. And for being there with Mom. Tell her I'll see her soon."

A woman's voice came on over the intercom to announce that boarding for her flight had begun.

"Gotta go. I'll call you later."

It was a typical red-eye with few people on board, but even with the entire row to herself and the lateness of the hour, Callie remained wide awake and restless. Her mother would be fine, she told herself. Broken bones could heal, and modern medicine would take good care of her. And Danny would see that she was being cared for properly. He had always been good at that, doing his best to fill the hole Elliot's death had left. The two of them had been more like brothers than best friends, and Danny's loyalty ran deep.

Callie leaned back against her headrest and stared out of the window beside her. There was nothing to see but darkness and her own reflection, so she turned away from it and closed her eyes, thinking about home. It would always be the only place she thought of as home, even though she had been in such a hurry to leave it. At eighteen, she had bypassed college and gone to LA for a while—much to her mother's horror—and from there she'd traveled up and down the coast of California, popping back home now and then to reassure her mother that she was still in one piece. They'd argued about it quite a bit: college was too important to skip, life on the road was no life for a girl her age, anything could happen to her...Her mother never ceased to come up with a reason why everything Callie wanted to do was a bad idea, but it hadn't stopped Callie from leaving.

Then there was a stretch in Mexico, followed by some time in Louisiana and Georgia. After that she headed north, and the visits and phone calls home had begun to grow fewer and farther between. The conversation was always the same, so it hardly seemed to matter if she called home less often. It only led to more frustration for both of them when she did, anyway.

Liddy had accused her once of leaving just to punish her for her decision to cut everything having to do with Callie's father out of their lives. That was not the reason why Callie had left, at least not consciously, but she knew Liddy didn't believe her. For someone who loved words so much, Callie had a hard time making other people understand why she couldn't bear to stay in one place for too long. Probably because she didn't fully understand it herself. She had met some fascinating people in the process, though, and found plenty of things about which to write.

She opened her eyes again. There was a man she had known in one of those places, one she'd allowed herself to get close to for a time, only to regret it. He had been hurt by the fact that she hadn't wanted him as much as he'd wanted her. She couldn't help it. Somehow, the men she met always fell short. Father issues? Or maybe it was something else. Maybe it was because none of them were Danny.

The last time she had seen Danny had been nearly four years ago. Thanksgiving.

She was in town to visit her mom for the holiday and to break the news that she was headed to the East Coast. Her mother was disappointed. So was Danny.

"So far away?" He had frowned at her. "Why? You hardly see your mom as it is. Family is important, Callie. Don't be so quick to take it for granted."

He disapproved, and she had resented that. So when she left, it was not under the happiest of circumstances, and she thought they both said things they regretted. She wasn't sure how it had escalated but suspected that her part in it had at least something to do with pent-up frustration over the fact that he persisted in seeing her as a kid instead of as a woman. Remembering it now, she smiled humorlessly. For someone who had wanted so badly to be seen as an adult, she behaved rather childishly, and she had spoken to him more harshly than she had intended. Maybe that was why she'd stayed away for so long.

Sighing, she deliberately turned her attention away from Danny and told herself to go to sleep.

But her mind was too busy to allow for much rest. By the time the final leg of her flights landed, Callie was bleary-eyed with exhaustion. She stumbled off the plane, considering her options. A cab would be the more comfortable way to get to the hospital since she could sleep in the back, but it would also cost a small fortune to travel that way over such a distance. A rental car made more sense, she supposed. Throwing her bag over her shoulder once more, she wearily trailed after other passengers through the gate. It had been a few years, but she thought she still remembered the way to the help desks.

"Callie?"

Hearing her name, she blinked in surprise and turned around.

A familiar figure stood off to one side of the crowd, hands tucked casually into the pockets of well-worn jeans as the throng of people jostled past him. In four years, he hadn't changed much, and he looked as much like a lean and tanned man of the outdoors as ever.

Funny how eight years could suddenly disappear and she was right back where she had been as a teenager, at a loss for words at the sight of him.

"Danny?" she managed finally, staring at him. "I—what are you doing here?"

He crossed through the crowd to get to her as easily as if he were crossing water. People just seemed to make way for him, some without even seeming to realize they were doing it. That was always the way with him. He didn't ooze the flashy sort of charm her brother had, the charm that always seemed to win Elliot hordes of female admirers, but Danny McCutcheon had an appeal all his own—one that radiated a quiet, solid sort of confidence.

And Danny had never lacked for female admirers either, much to Callie's teenage chagrin.

He stopped in front of her, his eyes taking her in and impossible for her to read. She felt flustered and had to resist the urge to duck her head as she might have done years ago. It had been a long time since she had trouble looking anybody in the eyes. "Thought you could use a ride," he said.

"Yeah, I could," she said awkwardly, torn between her pride and her sudden desire to throw her arms around him. It was so good to lay eyes on him again that it was almost painful. She hadn't realized how much she'd missed him until he was standing right in front of her. She wondered if he felt anything even remotely like that about her.

They couldn't stand there in the middle of the airport and just stare at each other forever, so finally she gave him a quick, one-armed hug that probably seemed too perfunctory and a little stiff, but it was too late to take it back. "It's good to see you, Danny."

He still smelled like the outdoors, and it still made her lightheaded.

She released him, and his hand brushed against her waist as they separated. "Been a while."

It might have been a rebuke, or it might have been a simple statement of fact. Apparently she had been away long enough to forget how to read him. "How's Mom doing?" she asked, changing the subject.

His face was a mask, expressionless as he studied her. "She's having surgery this morning. Probably be out of it by the time we get there."

"Surgery? For what?"

"She broke her hip. Doctor says if she can avoid infection, she should mend all right, though. She's going to need some looking after."

"I see."

He slipped the bag from her shoulder and put it over his own. "This it?"

"Yeah."

"We're out this way."

Without looking back, Danny led the way through the crowd of people and out to where his beat up old pickup truck sat.

Welcome home, Callie thought with a wistful pang as she followed him out.

• • •

Danny walked ahead of Callie to allow himself a few moments to absorb the impact of seeing her again. He hadn't expected it to hit him this hard, and he hoped it didn't show on his face.

He hardly recognized her. It wasn't that she looked very different. There were subtle changes, of course, some that he wasn't sure he could even put his finger on, but she still looked like Callie.

But she was different somehow. Older. Harder. Not the same girl he had known. She was a woman now, and she carried herself like one.

She also looked exhausted, Danny thought grimly, as he led the way among the parked cars. There were dark circles under her eyes, and she was much too pale. But then he had always thought that. A little sunshine and fresh air would do her a world of good compared to the smog of New York City. Other than that, though, she was as lean and lithe as ever.

He risked a backwards glance at her over his shoulder. She moved with a confident, sure stride that had not been there before, and when she caught him looking at her, she didn't look away first. He did.

Emotions warred within him. Relief at seeing her safe and sound after years away from home doing God knew what.

Bitterness at the easy way she seemed to cut him out of her life despite everything that should have linked them.

But he ought to have hugged her, a small voice inside him insisted. He ought to have held her and told her how good it was to have her back home instead of letting her get away with that aloof little one-armed excuse for a hug. It had been easy enough to do such things when she was his best friend's kid sister, but harder now. This woman walking with him seemed very different from that girl. He wasn't sure he knew her.

She smiled when she saw his truck, and it was a beautiful smile, one that made him suddenly nostalgic for older days when things were simpler between them. "Some things never change, do they?" she asked wryly, running a hand over a dent in the truck's fender, caused years ago in a misadventure with Elliot.

"Nothing wrong with that," he said more shortly than he'd intended.

Her smile faded, and he wanted to kick himself. He didn't want this visit to be a repeat of the last one, full of angry words and hurt feelings. There was a time, after Elliot's death, that he thought they might have been closer to each other than to anyone else. Maybe they would never be able to recapture the easy camaraderie that used to exist between them, but surely they could be civil to each other.

In an effort to be more conciliatory, he opened the passenger's side door for her and handed her the bag after she had settled into the seat. Then he closed the door and walked around to the driver's side, thinking that this might turn out to be a very long ride.

In the mood for more Crimson Romance?
Check out *Crashing the Congressman's Wedding*
by Elley Arden
at *CrimsonRomance.com*.

About the Author

Christine S. Feldman writes both novels and feature-length screenplays, and, to her great delight, she has placed in screenwriting competitions on both coasts. When she is not writing, she is teaching kindergarten, puttering around in her garden, ballroom dancing with her husband, or doing research for her next project.

www.ingramcontent.com/pod-product-compliance
Lightning Source LLC
Chambersburg PA
CBHW010639100726
47900CB00011B/2892